DEFENSE OF INNOCENTS

DON'T MISS THESE
ALEX ANDER THRILLERS!

Alex Ander writes what he enjoys reading – action thrillers packed with fistfights, gunfights, good-and-decent main characters, and heart-pounding excitement and adventure...all with clean language, no graphic sex, and an undertone of faith from a Christian worldview.

Aaron Hardy – Ex-Special Forces

The Unsanctioned Patriot

American Influence

Deadly Assignment

Patriot Assassin

The Nemesis Protocol

Necessary Means

Foreign Soil

Of Patriots and Tyrants

Act of Justice

The Last Kill

Two Minutes to War

Three Days in Rome

Dark Days of the Republic

Act of War

BIG SKY Series – Sheriff Wade Lockhart

Big Sky

Ambush

Reckoning

Jacob St. Christopher – Former FBI Hostage Rescue
Protect & Defend
Word of Honor
A Vow to the Innocent
Above & Beyond
Hard Road to Redemption

Jaxon Reigns – Ex-CIA Paramilitary Operations
To Reign Supreme
Hard Reign

Special Agent Cruz – FBI Agent
Vengeance is Mine
Defense of Innocents
Plea for Justice

Jessica Devlin – U.S. Marshal
Trust Fall
No Good Options
Let the Hunt Begin

Other Action Thrillers
Kill Order
Far From Mercy
Executive One Foxtrot

FREE Ebook
Escape & Evade
Go to AlexAnderNovelist.com

DEFENSE OF INNOCENTS

AN FBI THRILLER

ALEX ANDER

This book is a work of fiction. All names, characters, places and incidents are the products of the author's imagination or are used fictitiously. Any similarities to real events or locations or actual persons, living or dead, is entirely coincidental.

Copyright © 2025 by Jason A. Burley
All rights reserved

No portion of this publication may be reproduced or transmitted in any form or by any means without permission, except by a reviewer who may quote brief passages in a review to be published in a newspaper, magazine or electronically via the Internet.

TABLE OF CONTENTS

"Learn to do good; Seek justice,
Reprove the ruthless, Defend the orphan,
Plead for the widow."
- Isaiah Chapter 1; Verse 17

DEFENSE OF INNOCENTS

"If we keep to the starboard side and come in from the rear, we should be invisible. Brooks, I want you to lead Bravo Team. Enter the aircraft here through the rear-most door." Resting her foot on the front bumper of a black Chevy Tahoe, Special Agent Cruz leaned forward. Spread out on the hood of the vehicle was a drawing of a Boeing jet. She tapped a spot on the diagram. "Once you've gained entry, separate into two teams. One team clears the rear section, while the second team moves forward. When the plane is secure, I want all members of your team to stack up outside first class and wait for my order. You'll have one minute to get into position. *No one* breaches, until I give the command. Is that understood?"

"Roger that, ma'am," affirmed Brooks.

"The rest of us will comprise Alpha Team. Once we cross under the belly of the airplane, we'll ascend the stairs here," Cruz pointed at the map, "and hold position near the cockpit." She trained her finger on two men. "You and you hang back and secure both staircases." She twisted her torso. "You two are with Agent Ashford and me." The men nodded their assent.

Cruz removed her foot from the bumper and stood on the tarmac. Not wanting to spook the man they were preparing to apprehend, she had chosen to wear her street clothes—knee boots, jeans, sweater and overcoat. The two, four-man SWAT teams were dressed in black tactical gear.

Ashford had an FBI bulletproof vest over his street clothes. "I wish you'd reconsider and," he tucked his thumb under the vest and tugged, "put one of these under your sweater."

She shook her head. "I don't want him to see my bulging sweater and suspect something's wrong."

"He might just think you're a chunky gal and you could get away with it."

The other agents snickered.

She knew there was no malice in Ashford's comment, but she took the opportunity to send a playful shot across her partner's bow, backhanding him in the arm. "You'll regret that when this is over." Turning to the SWAT team members, she cautioned them. "Focus people. The target is highly skilled and trained by our very own U.S. Government. He's had three go-arounds in Iraq and Afghanistan, including the provinces of Helmand and Kandahar. I don't need to remind you those were deadly regions for our troops. After that, he appears to have become a ghost, suggesting Uncle Sam may have tapped him for more...*specialized*...missions." Cruz eyed each man. "Make no mistake, gentlemen. Our man needs no weapon. He *is* a weapon. Take nothing for granted and stay on high alert at all times."

One by one, the SWAT team members responded,

"Yes, ma'am."

"Remember," she tapped her chest, "I'm the one who makes first contact. No one does anything without my order." She looked at Ashford and lifted her eyebrows. He pursed his lips and shook his head. She went back to the SWAT team. "This operation should be over in less than three minutes from the time our boots hit the ground. The mobile stairs are already in place, so let's mount up and move out."

. . .

Cruz, Ashford and the SWAT team members stood in a line, stacked near the cockpit door, waiting for Bravo Team to get into position. She stole a glance beyond the opening that led to first class. She spotted her mark, sitting halfway back on the port side of the plane, her right. The flight attendant zipped by him. He leaned toward his window. Cruz looked further back when the blonde attendant slithered between the two drapes. She thought she had seen the helmet of one of the men from the second half of Bravo Team racing up the aisle. Lowering her gaze, she saw her target had returned to an upright position and was staring at her. *Crap!* She slowly leaned back behind concealment. *Did he make us?* Her earpiece crackled.

"Alpha, this is Bravo. We are in position, awaiting your order—over."

When the attendant was safely out of the way, Cruz would give the command; however, the woman never came into view. A few seconds passed. She heard a scuffle, followed by a muffled scream, and she leaned out again. The assailant had one arm enfolded around the attendant's neck, choking her, while pressing the handle of a silver spoon against her throat. He had not drawn blood, but the utensil was deep into the woman's neck. Cruz tapped her earpiece. "We've been made. All teams 'GO.' I repeat...Go—Go—Go!"

CHAPTER 2
TOWNHOUSE

March 20th, 1:32 p.m.
Vienna, Virginia
Two Days Earlier

FBI Special Agent Raychel Elisa DelaCruz climbed out of her black Dodge Charger and closed the door. She arched her back, cupping it in her hands. The forty-five minute drive from St. Matthew's Cathedral in Washington, D.C. had been frustrating. The day was gorgeous and it seemed everyone living between D.C. and Vienna had decided to enjoy the unseasonably warm temperatures and abundant sunshine by taking a Sunday afternoon drive. She leaned left and right, stretching her muscles. Standing straight, she tilted her head backward, closed her eyes and let the sun's rays warm her face. A few seconds later, she heard a low whistle followed by a familiar voice.

"So, this is how you dress when you're off the clock. You look nice, Cruz. I take it this is your Sunday best?" Those close to Special Agent DelaCruz called her Cruz, a shortened version of her name given to her when she was in the military. Her fellow soldiers had joked that her full name was too difficult to pronounce.

Cruz opened her eyes to see her partner, Special Agent Curtis Ashford, standing in front of the Charger.

He was dressed in a black suit, white shirt and black dress shoes. His red tie with blue diagonal pinstripes was held in place by a gold tie bar. With the sun behind him, his facial features were obscured in a shadowy blanket. She did not need the sun to see he was smiling. She knew by his tone of voice.

Ashford stood six-feet tall and weighed two hundred pounds. His black hair, dark eyes and long eyelashes gave him a hardened, yet attractive appearance. The square jaw and perpetual stubble on his cheeks took his 'bad boy' good looks to a higher level. He had an athletic frame with wide shoulders, a narrow waist and heavily muscled arms and legs. A football player in college, he made the team as a linebacker. A few practices later, his coaches moved him to running back, where he ran over and through defenders on his way to a school rushing record in his first year. A knee injury in the playoffs ended his college career and derailed his professional football hopes.

Drawing her long and dark brown hair into a mid-rise ponytail, Cruz glanced at her clothes. She wore a matching red suit coat and knee-length pencil skirt that hugged every curve of her well-toned five-foot, eight-inch figure. Below her bare legs, she had on a pair of two-inch high-heel red pumps. A white button-up blouse completed her outfit. She secured the ponytail and smiled. "You could say that." She pointed her chin toward the dwelling Ashford had exited. "So, what do we have here?"

Ashford pivoted and led the way into the 1,200 square-foot townhouse at the end of Oakdale Woods Court. Hardwood floors throughout the structure with crown molding and a private rear patio, the $400,000 home had two levels with spacious bedrooms, two baths and plenty of attic space for storage. The residence was beautiful by any standard. The owners had good taste and good jobs to afford the luxurious amenities.

Ashford and Cruz passed through the living room and entered the kitchen where the first body, a lump covered by a white sheet, lay between the kitchen table and the entryway into the living room. A red streak ran from the edge of the sheet toward the living room. The kitchen was neat and tidy. One spoon lay on the floor near the refrigerator, its door slightly ajar. All the chairs were pushed under the table, except for one. The back of that chair was against the counter halfway between the sink and the refrigerator.

Ashford got the attention of a man standing near the body and made introductions. "Detective Reynolds, this is Special Agent DelaCruz." He motioned toward the detective and glanced at Cruz. "This is Detective Reynolds. He's in charge of the investigation."

Reynolds shook Cruz's hand. "Thank you for coming, Agent DelaCruz." He flicked his eyes toward Ashford. "As I said to your partner, from the looks of what we've got here, we sure could use the resources the FBI can bring to bear in this case." He paused and studied the white sheet. "I haven't seen anything like it in my ten years as a detective."

Short, pudgy and standing three inches shy of Cruz's height, Detective Mark Reynolds was forty-two years old. Brown hair covered his round head. The beginnings of a receding hairline testified to his age. Deep horizontal lines showed on his forehead. Below the lines, thick and bushy eyebrows rested above deeply set eyes. When he spoke, his nostrils flared and the dark mustache under his wide nose moved up and down.

Cruz stepped away from the detective and sat on her haunches in front of the victim. She lifted the sheet. Lifeless eyes stared back at her. She took special note of the multiple gunshot wounds before shutting her eyes and lowering her head. *Lord, grant him peace and eternal rest. In Jesus' name, I pray. Amen.* She gave the man's body another onceover and eased the sheet to the floor with both hands.

Ashford had been hovering over her. "Did you notice the GSW's?"

Knowing the lingo for gunshot wounds, Cruz concurred, "Two to the body...one to the head."

"Do you think it's a coincidence?"

She glanced over her shoulder at the ransacked living room. "Well, if this wasn't a home invasion, then someone went to a lot of trouble to make it look that way."

Ashford poked a finger at the sheet. "Thugs don't shoot like that."

Her knees together, Cruz pushed on them and stood. Adjusting her skirt, she mulled her partner's words.

Reynolds agreed. "The wife's body is upstairs and has the same pattern—double tapped in the chest and a single shot in her forehead. That's what made me think to call you. These look like professional hits."

She turned her attention to the sheet, her mind visualizing the body. A contract killing changed the dynamics of the case. Armed robbers, home invaders sought money, jewelry, electronic devices. The motivations for their actions were easier to determine. Professional killers, however, complicated the investigation. They worked for other people, adding another layer of complexity. No, she was not ready to pursue the possibility of a professional hit. She raised her head toward Reynolds. "I'd like to see the other body."

. . .

After examining the other victim and inspecting the rummaged rooms on the second floor, Cruz, Ashford and Reynolds returned to the kitchen. Hands on her hips and scanning the room, she stood near the table; on the opposite side laid the body. "What have you learned about the victims, detective?"

Detective Reynolds studied his notepad. "Jason and Jane Wilson...age forty and thirty-eight...they both worked at a pharmaceutical company in nearby

Reston...research scientists...been married for ten years with one child, a daughter."

Cruz remembered seeing photos of a little girl. One of the bedrooms was decorated in a girl's theme—pink walls, ponies and princesses. She spied a child's handheld video game on the kitchen table. "How old is the daughter?"

"According to what we've been able to dig up so far," he paused to flip a few pages, "she should be around seven years old."

Frowning, Cruz glanced at the detective out of the corner of her eye. "Where is she?"

Reynolds shook his head. "We don't know. She wasn't here if that's what you're getting at. My men have searched every floor and every room of this place. There are signs a small child lives here, but the child wasn't found."

Ashford analyzed his partner. Her face seemed to be aging by the second. "Detective, do you know if the Wilson's have family in the area?"

"As we speak, we're trying to track down the next of kin. We're also checking with the neighbors to see if they know any friends of the Wilson's, in case the girl may be at a friend's house."

Cruz turned away. Placing her interlocked fingers on her head, she gazed at nothing in particular. Her heart was racing. *Was the girl here when her parents were murdered? Did she see it happen? Did the killers see her and take her? Did they—* Cruz could not finish the last thought. *Dear God, let her be okay. Let her be safe and help us find her, Lord.* She spun on her heels and put her hands on her hips. Staring at the table, she envisioned the worst, while listening to Reynolds finish bringing her and Ashford up to speed on the details of the case. She observed the video game. Her eyes never straying from it, she extended her hand toward the men. "I need a rubber glove?"

Reynolds hailed an officer. Moments later, he handed Cruz two rubber gloves. "What is it?"

She donned the gloves and picked up the game. After examining the screen, she pressed one of the console's buttons a few times and shot a look toward the detective. "What was the Wilson's time of death?"

Reynolds licked his finger and swiped it across pages in his notepad. "I have an *estimated* time of death between 6 p.m. and midnight."

"Detective, have any of your men touched this game...played with it or," she swirled her open hand above the device, "done *anything* with it?"

He shook his head. "No, that's not how we do things. My officers are only to secure the scene. The people from the crime lab collect the evidence." He jerked his thumb over his shoulder. "The lab techs arrived right before you. I told them to stay away from the rooms with the bodies, until you had had a chance to see everything for yourself."

Cruz's eyebrows rolled inward. Creases formed on her forehead.

"What's going on, Agent DelaCruz?"

"What time did the first officer arrive on the scene?"

Reynolds checked his notes and replied, "8:58 a.m."

Placing the game on the table, she inspected the room. From a new perspective, her eyes took in every detail of the kitchen—the spoon on the floor, the chair against the counter, the open refrigerator door, a box of cereal on the counter in front of the chair. She tipped her head backward and saw a half-open cupboard door, revealing more cereal boxes. The color drained from her cheeks and her eyes widened. "The girl's in the house—*right now*." Cruz waved her arms. "Have your men spread out and search the house...go over every square inch of this place...open every door, every closet...search every shelf—"

Reynolds interrupted. "What makes you so sure she's here?"

She pointed at the game. "The last three high scores have today's date. The most recent one has a time stamp of 8:55 a.m., *three minutes* before the first officer showed up."

Ashford pointed at the game. "Those dates and times could be off, Cruz."

"Maybe," she said.

Reynolds shook his head. "I told you, we've gone over every room. There's no little girl."

Cruz rolled her eyes and sighed. "Think back to your childhood, detective. Did you ever play hide and seek? I did. And, I found some *small* places to hide." She held her praying hands in front of her chest. "Please humor me. Have your men—"

"I got it. I got it." Reynolds rushed into the living, issuing commands to his officers.

Cruz motioned. "We'll start in the kitchen." She pointed toward Ashford's half of the room. "Take that side. I'll start here." They moved toward each other, opening and closing every door. Coming to where the counter made a right angle, Cruz pulled on a double-hinged door. Two sections opened to form a wide door. Struggling in her tight-fitting skirt, she went to one knee before bending at the waist and peering inside the darkened cavity. She squinted. Once her eyes adjusted to the dimness, she clutched her chest and gasped.

Her body pressed against the back corner of the cabinet, Madison did not budge, did not breathe. She kept her eyes open as long as she could, afraid the movement of her eyelids would give away her presence to the dark-haired, dark-eyed woman. Staring at her, the woman looked a lot like Madison's mother, long and curly eyelashes, high cheekbones and not a single blemish on her face. The thought refreshed the memories of her mother's screams. Screams that fell silent after the sound of three muffled pops. The pops sounded the same as the two she had heard before her father tumbled to the floor. Lying on his back, he had motioned with his eyes toward her secret hiding place. Understanding the cue, she scampered into the corner space, closed the door and peeked through a gap in the frame. A tall man, dressed in black, entered the kitchen and stood over her pleading father. She did not see the pistol, but she heard a crack, louder than the first two sounds. Her father's begging stopped and his arms dropped to the floor.

Seeing the scene play out in her mind, Madison closed her eyes. If she remained motionless and silent, she hoped the woman would leave her alone. Her lungs were burning. Pressure was building in her head. She needed to take a breath, but she held off for several more seconds, until the woman spoke to her.

Special Agent Cruz recoiled at the sight of the little girl jammed into the corner of the cabinet, her knees against her chest, arms wrapped around her legs. Her blonde hair came to her shoulders in back. The bangs in front stopped at her eyebrows. Beneath those eyebrows were the most beautiful eyes, round and bright blue. Cruz had never seen such pretty eyes on a girl. Bulging, they never wavered. Cruz averted her gaze. A blanket was spread over the floor of the cabinet. To her right, a spoon rested in an empty bowl. Picture books littered the area at the girl's feet. To the left, a few small kitchen appliances and a box of plastic wrap lined the side of the cabinet. If it were not for the grisly circumstances, this space was a cozy getaway for any child.

Cruz recovered from her initial shock and flashed her warmest, friendliest smile. "Hello." No greeting was returned. Not that she was expecting one. The kid was terrified. To her, every adult in the house was a danger. Cruz lowered her other knee to the floor and sat on her heels. "You've got a nice little fort here. Did you make this yourself?" No response came. *That's okay. I'll carry the conversation.* "Do you mind if I come in?" Cruz threw back the lapels of her suit coat and slithered out of the garment, letting it fall to the floor. Removing her paddle holsters, one for her Glock 23 and one for two spare magazines, she handed them to Ashford.

Getting into the tight space wearing a pencil skirt

        DEFENSE OF INNOCENTS

was no small feat. Cruz's figure may have been slim, but the cabinet was slimmer. Lying on her left side and propped on her elbow, she interlocked her fingers in front of her belly. The girl was within arm's reach. Cruz smiled. *Let's try this again.* "My name's Raychel. What's your name?" Moments of stillness passed. She reached for a book and the girl dug the heels of her bare feet into the wooden surface, driving her body backward. Seeing terror in the child's eyes, Cruz yanked her hand back. "It's okay, sweetie. I'm not going to hurt you. You're safe, I promise." Her words did not stop the attempt to escape through the hardwood cabinet panel. "It's okay. We can just sit here." She folded her hands and tried to scoot further away, but her back was touching the appliances. *This isn't going as well as I'd hoped it would.*

After several minutes of a one-way conversation, Cruz felt a hand engulf her knee. She turned her head to see a second hand holding the video game that had been on the kitchen table. She recognized the well-manicured fingernails. *Good thinking, Ash.* She took the device and intentionally held it upside down between her and the girl. "Look what my friend just gave me." She glanced up and saw the girl's eyes quickly flash from Cruz to the game before settling back on Cruz. This was the first time the girl had taken her eyes off Cruz, signaling a miniscule breakthrough. Pressing buttons, she feigned incompetence. "I've never been good at these games." She kept hitting buttons. Buzzing noises sounded from the console's speakers, culminating in a dreadful song, designed to let the user know the game was finished. Cruz messed with the game and the song played three more times. Before the song had stopped playing for the third time, she heard a soft and quiet voice.

"You're doing it wrong." Madison moved closer to Cruz, but quickly returned to the corner when she realized she had spoken her thoughts.

"Really," questioned Cruz. "What am I doing wrong?" She held out the game. "Can you show me how to play this? I'll bet you're good at it. I see someone with the initials M.W. has the highest score. Is that you?" The girl barely moved her head up and down. "My initials are R.D. They stand for Raychel DelaCruz. What do your initials stand for?"

Nearly a minute passed before the girl whispered, "Madison." Moments later, her voice went up an octave and she said, "Madison Wilson." The girl's shoulders dropped. Up to this point, they had been frozen in a permanent shrug.

Cruz watched the kid's eyes dart left, right, up and down. She could almost see the little one's mind scanning the new arrival and assessing the risk factor. She had gotten by the child's outer defenses, but there was a lot of territory yet to cover. "It's nice to meet you, Madison."

Madison slid closer to Cruz. "Mommy and Daddy call me Maddie."

"Maddie is a pretty name."

"Everyone else calls me Madison."

Cruz smiled. "Well, I'll be sure to call you—"

Madison stuck out a finger. "You can call me Maddie, just like Mommy and Daddy."

Cruz's throat tightened. "Thank you, Maddie." She cleared her throat. "You can call me Raychel."

For the next thirty minutes, Madison played her game, intermittently pausing to point at the screen and the score. Cruz nodded and showed interest the girl's ability. She noted that the girl was indeed good at playing the game.

When the end-of-game song started to play, Madison dropped the device into her lap and exaggerated a sigh. "I died."

Cruz craned her head to see the screen. "But, you got a really high score again. I'll *never* be as good as you." Silence consumed the small space. Madison had retreated to an upright fetal position. "What's wrong, Maddie?" *What's wrong, Maddie? Dumb question, Raychel. What isn't wrong?* The little girl's next words came out of her mouth as a whisper.

"Mommy and Daddy are dead, too, aren't they?"

The lump in Cruz's throat returned as a stranglehold. She opened her mouth to speak, but nothing came out. She swallowed hard and stared at Madison. Her tone gentle and even, Cruz replied, "Yes, Maddie, they are." Fighting to hold back the tears at the corners of her eyes, she pushed her body away from the appliances. Having fallen asleep for the third time in the last half hour, her left leg would not cooperate. The shoulder that had been supporting her was stiff, and she almost rolled and fell flat on her face. Slowly straightening her left arm, she wrapped it around the girl and held her close, kissing the top of Madison's head. "You don't have to be afraid. I'm here and I promise you—you're safe. No one is going to lay a finger on you." The sobbing and the shaking body in her arms pierced Cruz's heart, sending streams of liquid down her cheeks.

Ashford had been listening to the entire conversation. He turned and swiped a hand across his face. He approached Detective Reynolds and spoke to the man in a hushed tone. "You should put in a call to social services and get a counselor out here." He tilted his head toward the cabinet. "If she's witnessed any of what's happened here, she's going to need some help."

"I've already made the call, Agent Ashford. They're on their way."

"What about the next of kin? Where do we stand on that?"

"We've contacted the grandparents. They're driving up from Florida to take custody of the girl. Until they arrive, a social worker will care for her."

. . .

For ten minutes, Cruz hugged Madison, stroking her hair. Gradually, the sobbing became whimpering and the whimpering morphed into sporadic, short breaths. She used her fingers in place of a tissue and dared to speak. "Are—" she cleared her throat, "Are you feeling better, Maddie?" Madison's nodding head rubbed against Cruz's chin. "I'm glad to hear it. What do you say we go get something to eat? I'm hungry. Are you hungry?" Right on cue, her stomach rumbled.

A grin on her face, Madison shot Cruz a look. "You farted."

Cruz chuckled. "No, I didn't. That was my stomach. I'm hungry."

Not convinced, the girl squinted. Still squinting, she cocked her head and held the woman's gaze for several seconds before jutting out her finger toward the kitchen. "You're not like the others. You care about Mommy and Daddy."

Cruz pulled her head away from the girl to look her square in the eye. "No, Maddie, we *all* care about—"

"I saw you with my Daddy. Your lips were moving, but you didn't say anything."

Recalling what the girl was referring to, Cruz nodded her head. "I was praying for your Dad."

"What did you say?"

Cruz rolled her eyes upward. "I...I asked Jesus to give your Dad peace."

Madison touched the gold crucifix hanging from the gold chain around Cruz's neck and said, "Jesus?"

"That's right, Jesus. He loves your parents very much and He's taking care of them right now."

Cupping the jewelry, the girl pulled it closer, stopping short of putting tension on the fine chain. "Did you pray for Mommy?"

"Yes, I did."

"What did you say?"

Cruz grinned. *So this is what it's like to be on the other end of an interrogation.* "I asked Jesus to take care of your Mommy...and to take care of you, too." She poked the girl's stomach, eliciting a giggle. "Do you like pizza?"

Madison nodded her head, her attention returning to the crucifix.

"Me, too," said Cruz, reaching behind her and unhooking the chain. "I like ham and pineapple on my pizza." She swung the necklace in front of Madison before pulling back on the ends and connecting them behind the girl's neck. "What do you like on *your* pizza?"

Madison dropped her chin and lifted the jewelry. She whipped her head around, gaping at Cruz with arched eyebrows.

Cruz nodded. "That's yours now." The girl beamed. "We're friends, right?" Nodding, the child's body rocked back and forth. "Well, friends do stuff like that for each other. They give each other gifts." She tapped the crucifix. "That's a gift from me to you."

Madison let go of the crucifix, twisted her body and threw her arms around the neck of her new friend.

Cruz winced when a sharp corner of an appliance dug into her back. The joy from the simple act, however, more than compensated for the pain. Cradling the tiny head in one hand, she returned the hug and kissed Madison's cheek. "Now, how about we get some pizza?"

With help from Ashford, Special Agent Cruz wiggled out from the confines of the cabinet. She instructed him to stand in front of the body on the kitchen floor. There was no need for Madison to see the sheet-covered lump. Standing, she held out her hands. "Come to me." The girl crawled out and came to her. Cruz ushered her toward the archway between the kitchen and the pantry. Holding the girl at her side, she faced Ashford. Detective Reynolds had joined her partner and the two of them made a wall in front of the body. Cruz needed answers, but she did not want to subject Madison to the specifics of the case. She lifted her head toward the two men, her eyes darting back and forth between them.

Ashford whispered. "Grandparents are coming from Florida. ETA is the early morning hours." He glanced at the child firmly attached to Cruz. "Social worker will be here for her."

Cruz nodded and looked at Madison. "We're getting out of here," she came back to the men, "to get something to eat."

Detective Reynolds shook his head. "You can't do that Agent Cruz. Social Services will be here shortly." Hearing a commotion behind him, he looked over his shoulder. "In fact, they're here now."

A woman dressed in a gray business suit appeared from behind Reynolds. Her dark hair was formed into a ball on top of her head. Oversized wire-rimmed glasses took up too much of her face. Her lips pressed together and her eyebrows joining at the bridge of her nose, she plopped a briefcase onto the kitchen table. "I'm Clarissa. I'm here for the child." She jabbed a finger at Madison. "Is that her? What's her name?" The woman flicked the latches on the briefcase and opened the lid. Pulling out a thick stack of papers and dropping them onto the table, she repeated the question. "I said...what's the name? I need to get started on the paperwork." She spun her head and body to her left and addressed Reynolds. "I understand the grandparents are coming for the subject. When will they be here?"

Reynolds replied, "Sometime after midnight."

Clarissa rolled her eyes, sighed and mumbled. "Okay, let's get this over with." She pulled out a chair and sat.

Squinting, Cruz regarded the woman, not knowing what to make of her. *Subject? Who refers to a child as a subject? Is this a joke? Who in their right mind would let this woman anywhere near a child?* Cruz felt ten razor-like fingernails slicing into the tender part of her inner thigh. The girl had shoved her hands under Cruz's skirt and was clutching her leg with every ounce of strength she had. *Thank God, it's not the left one.* Tingling sensations were slowly receding in that leg. She put a gentle hand on the shoulder of her new appendage.

Clarissa beckoned toward Madison. "All right, come here. I need to have a look at you."

Madison's nails dug in deeper.

Cruz sucked in a short breath and listed to her right.

A high-pitched squeal filled the room. "No, don't let her take me, Raychel. I don't want to go with her." The shrieking plea drew sympathy from the two men. Reynolds turned his head and rubbed the back of his neck. Ashford crossed his arms and stared at the floor.

Sliding her hands down her thigh, Cruz wedged them under the skinny arms, breaking the hold. "It's okay, sweetie," she whispered, picking up the girl and holding her on her hip. Madison wrapped her arms around Cruz's neck and whirled her face away from the social worker. Cruz glanced sideways, her stare penetrating to the back of the state employee's head.

Repeatedly tapping her pen on the table, the scowling woman let out a heavy sigh, ending in a low groan. "Bring the girl to me. I need to check for injuries, marks." When her command was not heeded, she tossed her pen onto the table and growled, "Oh, for—" The social worker flapped her open hands toward her chest. "Bring her here. I don't *bite*."

Cruz heard the sting in the woman's voice. Madison did too. The girl flinched and Cruz lightly patted the child's back. *I'm not so sure of that.* Pinching her lower lip between her teeth, she shifted her gaze back and forth from Ashford to the social worker three or four times.

On her last pass toward her partner, she paused and held his gaze. His face deadpan, he dipped his chin slowly and brought it back up. The gesture strengthened her resolve.

Cruz tilted her head and whispered into Madison's ear. "No one's taking you anywhere, Maddie. I won't let them." She locked eyes with Clarissa and forced a smile. "Thank you for your time, ma'am, but I will be caring for the child, until the grandparents get here."

Both Detective Reynolds and the woman replied in unison. "You can't do that."

Clarissa went further. "You are not qualified to take custody. We can't just let her go with *anyone*. We have policies and procedures for cases like these. I'm afraid until the next of kin are able to—"

Her voice deeper, Cruz interrupted. "Perhaps, I'm not making myself *perfectly* clear." She pivoted to her right, placing more of her body between Madison and the woman. Cruz's jaw muscles tightened. "You are *not* coming anywhere *near* this young lady."

Clarissa leaned back in her chair. Her eyes grew wide and a space opened between her lips. "Excuse me? Are you refusing the power of the State?" She rocked forward and pushed herself to a standing position.

Cruz lowered Madison to the floor, positioning the child behind her body.

Clarissa folded her arms. "Agent DelaCruz is it? You're out of line. You have no authority in this matter." She lowered her head. "I strongly suggest you step aside and let me handle this."

Cruz squinted and squared her shoulders. "And, I suggest you stand down before you get hurt."

Ashford uncrossed his arms, but held them in front of his body. Perspiration formed on his forehead and he swallowed.

The woman twisted her head and peered at her female adversary through one eye. "Are you threatening me, Agent DelaCruz?"

Out of the corner of his eye, Ashford saw Reynolds open his mouth. He crossed in front of the man, showing him his palm. Stepping between the women, he faced the social worker. "You should know never to come between a mother and her cub." He let his words hang in the air. "Now *back...off.*"

Reading Ashford's intentions, the woman's jaw slackened. Her eyes reduced to slits, she gaped at Cruz for several moments before her chest dropped and a breath of air escaped her lungs. *Forget it. This isn't worth it.* She spun on her heels, stuffed papers into her briefcase and slammed shut the lid. "This is not over. I'll be filing a report." Storming out of the kitchen, she wagged her finger. "You have *not* heard the last from me."

Cruz bent around Ashford and shouted. "Special Agent DelaCruz...*capital D...capital C...*Make sure you spell it correctly."

Ashford met his partner and pumped his hands toward her chest. "Take it easy, Cruz. No one is taking the girl. If they try," he swung his finger back and forth between them, "they'll have to go through *both* of us."

She exhaled noisily through pressed lips.

He smiled at Madison, peeking out from around Cruz's body. "Take her outside." He tipped his head backward and lowered his voice. "I'll smooth things over with Reynolds and meet you at your car."

"Thanks, Ash."

. . .

With Cruz's red jacket draped over his arm, Ashford strode down the sidewalk, meeting her a few feet from the front bumper of the Charger.

Cruz motioned toward the townhouse, while taking the jacket. "How'd it go in there?"

Ashford puckered his lips and tilted his head. "Reynolds is not happy."

"I don't care. I did—"

Ashford held up his hand. "Let me finish."

She slid her arms into the sleeves of her jacket, popped out her ponytail and reclaimed her holsters from him.

"He's not happy, but he sees the bigger picture. I don't blame him. I'd feel the same way if I were in his shoes. He has someone he answers to as well. Frankly, I'm surprised he didn't send a couple officers out here to retrieve the girl." Ashford put his hands on his hips. "However, he saw the bond you established with her and is willing to look the other way," he tilted his head backward, "over what happened in there. I believe his words were...'The kid's been through hell...Why take her security blanket, too?'" He poked a finger in her direction and added, "Meaning *you*."

Cruz affixed the holsters to the waistband of her skirt. "Good. I'm glad he gets it."

"Yeah, but I'm not quite sure I get it."

She lifted her head. "What do you mean?"

Ashford stared beyond her shoulder at the vehicle and the girl inside. "What's your plan here, Cruz? I backed you up in there with Social Services and Reynolds, because you're my partner." He looked her in the eyes. "Tell me where this is going. I check my email daily and I don't remember reading anything about the FBI getting into the babysitting business. What am I missing?"

"She's innocent in all this, Ash—defenseless." Cruz pointed toward the townhouse. "Reynolds hit the nail on the head. She needs some sense of stability in her life. God only knows the horrors she's witnessed. The girl crawled into that cabinet, because she felt safe in there. And, the only reason she came out was she trusted and felt safe with," Cruz jerked her thumb toward her chest, "*me*." Crossing her arms and shifting her weight to one foot, she added, "I'm *not* going to abandon her."

Cupping his right elbow in his left hand, Ashford stroked his chin and stared at the pavement. On several occasions during their time together, she had displayed this level of determination, defiance. *She's digging in her heels.* Nothing he could say would change her mind. He glimpsed the red pumps on her feet and inwardly laughed at the unintended pun. "Reynolds has one condition. He wants to know the girl's whereabouts at all times. And, when the grandparents come to take her—"

Cruz lifted her hands. "I'll be more than willing to surrender her to them."

Ashford nodded. "All right, then. I guess we can add...*Defense of Innocents* to our job descriptions."

She smiled. "I like the sound of that."

He directed his thumb toward the townhouse. "I'm going back in and getting every scrap of information I can from Reynolds. Are you going straight home?"

"Yes," Cruz turned and beckoned him to follow, "after we stop for pizza." She opened the lid of the Charger's trunk. Grabbing her overnight bag, she emptied the contents and handed it to him. "Take some clothes for Madison—pajamas, socks, underwear, the usual stuff and bring them to the house. I've got nothing for little girls."

"Okay."

She snapped her fingers. "Get some toys, too."

"Sure."

Cruz slammed the trunk lid and turned before spinning around. "She likes books and video games. Maybe get some—"

"I can handle it, Cruz."

She gestured toward the dwelling with her chin. "If Reynolds gives you any crap about removing evidence, just buy everything at the store and I'll pay you back."

Ashford chuckled and shook his head. He grasped her shoulders to get her to stand still. Her mind was going in several different directions. "Cruz," he pointed through the back window of her vehicle. "You take care of *her*." He placed his open hand on his chest. "I'll take care of the rest. You need to be there for her physically *and* mentally."

She focused on him, letting his words roll around in her brain. Sometimes, the simplest advice was the most valuable. "You're right." She pretended to hold a phone to her face. "Call me when you have something."

"I'll do better than that. Once I get a bag packed and have all the details of the case, I'll bring everything to the house." He cranked his head toward the car. "Go...I've got it from here."

Cruz thanked her partner and climbed into the Charger. Madison was buckled in her seat. Cruz smiled. "Are you ready to go?"

Madison returned the gesture. "Where are we going for pizza?"

Cruz pursed her lips and closed one eye. She glanced at the clock on the dashboard (3:15) before coming back to her passenger and saying, "I know a perfect place near Washington, D.C."

Special Agent Cruz lived in a beautiful home located at the end of Cripplegate Road in Potomac, Maryland. The traditional two-story all brick center hall colonial home sat on nearly two acres of private land, a short distance from the Potomac River. Forest green shutters on either side of the windows accented the red brick, and the white house trim seemed to offset the home's lavishness and create a more basic and down to earth feel for the occupants. A large and striking bow window was centered in the front of the house. An attached two-car garage was on the right side of the house. On the left, a patio with glass windows on three sides overlooked the wooded property.

The inside of the home was equally beautiful; hardwood floors throughout, four bedrooms, four full-size bathrooms, a fireplace on the main floor and a second fireplace in the upstairs master bedroom. A wooden staircase, leading to the second floor, bisected the main floor. The main floor consisted of a living room with a fireplace, a large kitchen and dining area, two bathrooms and a combined library and den. The second floor had four bedrooms and two bathrooms.

Cruz was extremely fortunate to be living in this home in one of the most affluent towns in the United States. The home was owned by an elderly man who had lost his wife a few years ago. The couple owned a real estate company and had amassed a small fortune, including several homes scattered throughout the country. After his wife had passed, he moved to a warmer climate in the Southwest. Cruz had met him through a friend of hers. He did not want to sell the property, because it held special memories for him and his late wife. He had been searching for someone he could trust to live in it for a greatly reduced monthly rent. After a luncheon meeting with Cruz, he offered her the home on the spot.

Having already seen the home and the neighborhood, Cruz could not pass up the generous offer. The man had two conditions. One, she was required to maintain the home. If anything needed to be repaired, she was to take care of it and send him the bill. He would pay for all repairs. Two, the home's furnishings were never to be moved. She could use anything she wanted, but the home was to stay the same. She could have personal items as long as they could be easily removed.

Driving away from the townhouse in Vienna, Cruz had negotiated with Madison, postponing the promise of pizza until dinner. They stopped for a quick bite to quell their hunger pangs before heading to a park a couple miles from Cruz's home. The girl needed some time to be a kid and play. They spent the next hour frolicking on the playground equipment. It had been more than two decades since the twenty-nine-year-old woman had swung on a child's swing set. Kicking her feet, the technique came back to her. At one point, she swung her legs hard enough to throw one of her high heels across the playground. Madison got such a thrill from the accident that Cruz intentionally let the second shoe fly. The little girl giggled with delight.

Once home, the duo created a ham, pepperoni and pineapple pizza from scratch, which included making the dough from flour. After she had closed the oven door and set the timer, Cruz pinched some leftover flour between her fingers and flicked it at the girl. Madison flinched, but recovered when she saw the playful grin on Cruz's face. Not understanding the art of a pinch, the girl scooped up two handfuls and tossed them at the older woman.

Covered in powder and laughing, Cruz regretted her decision to instigate the flour fight, quickly calling for a cease-fire. After brushing off their clothing, the two retreated to the living room to watch television.

Sitting on the couch, her feet pressed against her butt, Cruz had her arm around the girl, snuggling with her under a fleece blanket. A children's movie played on the television. Madison's eyes were fixated on the screen. Periodically, she would look up and smile before wiggling back into a comfortable position.

Cruz played with the girl's soft and wispy hair. *How is she going to handle this when she fully understands what happened? Her parents are dead and she will never see them again in this life.* She cocked her head and regarded the girl. She wished she could do something to make things better. Nothing could be done. The best she could do was pray for her. Hopefully, the tragedy would not scar her for the rest of her life. The timer sounded.

Madison pulled away and twisted her body.

Her eyes wide and mouth open, Cruz tickled the girl. "I think it's ready. Are you hungry?" Madison leaped off the couch. "Okay, I'll take that as a 'yes.'" She hit the 'pause' button on the remote and threw off the blanket. "Let's eat."

A few minutes later, a piece of homemade pizza was in their hands. "Well," said Cruz, putting the slice on her plate. "Was it worth the wait?" Sitting on a barstool drawn up to the island in the center of the kitchen, Madison chewed and nodded. The doorbell rang. Grabbing a napkin, Cruz slid off her barstool. "You keep eating and I'll see who's here."

Wiping her hands, she peered through the peephole in the front door before opening the door. "Come on in, Ash."

He tilted his head back and pointed his nose in different directions. "What smells so good in here? Is that pizza? I thought you were having that for lunch."

She closed the door. "Change of plans. We made homemade pizza for dinner. Are you hungry?" She cocked her head toward the kitchen and took a couple steps. "We made plenty."

Ashford caught her by the arm. "Hold on." He set Cruz's overnight bag on the floor, leaned left and saw Madison at the island. Lowering his voice, he produced a notepad from his jacket pocket. "I want to bring you up to speed first." He opened the notepad. "Jason and Jane Wilson were research scientists, working for one of the top pharmaceutical companies in the nation, Payne Laboratories, headquartered in Reston, Virginia. Henry Payne is the president and CEO of the company, which has been on the Fortune 100 list since its inception. They've manufactured and brought to market more than fifty drugs ranging from cholesterol and blood pressure medicine to vitamin supplements. Their most recent product has shown results in slowing the growth of cancer cells."

Cruz turned her head and stared at the floor. "Payne...Why does that name sound familiar?"

"It should," said Ashford, flipping a page. "Henry Payne is the younger brother of Senator Walter Payne from Virginia."

Two years ago, Senator Payne ran for President of the United States. He shepherded a hard-fought campaign, filled with the worst mudslinging in recent decades. The nonstop television ads reeked of negativity and bordered on the verge of slander. In the end, the people preferred a two-term Governor from Massachusetts, James Conklin, who had served in the Marines. While stationed in Beirut in 1983, he was wounded when a suicide bomber detonated a truck bomb near the building serving as the barracks.

Cruz snapped her fingers. "That's where I recognize the name." She motioned toward Ashford's notepad. "What else have you got?"

"Not much. The lab is still working on processing fingerprints. The neighbors don't remember seeing anyone entering or exiting the building around the time of the murders." He turned back a few pages. "This is odd, however." He thumped the pad. "There were security cameras on both floors that covered most of the townhouse. It was a closed-circuit system, hardwired back to a small closet in the master bedroom."

Cruz lifted her head to look him in the eye. "What did it capture? Do we have the killer on video?"

Ashford shook his head. "There was no computer or laptop found at the end of the cabling. The cable had been cut and was lying on the floor."

Cruz scrunched up her face. "What," she said? She showed him her palms. "Where was the computer?"

"The police haven't found any computers. Plus, the cell phones for the victims had been taken. There's no digital footprint left in that house."

"Was anything of value taken?"

       DEFENSE OF INNOCENTS

He shrugged. "That's hard to say," he stole a glance toward the kitchen, and the little girl, "without the parents alive to tell us. We can speculate that money and valuables were taken, but…"

Cruz faced the kitchen and crossed her arms. She had not wanted to pull the trigger on the murders being a professional hit; however, add this new information to the bullet wound pattern on the victim's bodies and she was a step closer to drawing that conclusion. If this was not a burglary gone awry, then who wanted a couple of scientists dead, and why? Cruz rubbed her forehead before running her hand down her face.

"Whoever did this were pros, Cruz. I know you have your doubts, but this just isn't adding up to robbery. We'll know more in the morning when fingerprint results come in, but I doubt they'll be much help." Ashford wagged his finger. "I forgot to tell you. Both victims were shot with a twenty-two. Even dumb robbers know enough to use a larger caliber weapon. No, the more I think about this, my gut tells me the killer, or killers, were on the offensive. They knew their targets. They sneaked into the house with silenced weapons, and executed a plan—pros."

Cruz pressed her lips together and drew in a deep breath through her nose. She held the air for a few seconds before letting it out through drawn lips. Blinking several times, she ran her fingers through the length of her hair. "Thanks, Ash." She motioned toward the kitchen. "Let's put on happy faces. She's been traumatized enough for one day. Are you staying for pizza?"

He slipped his fingers inside the handle of the overnight bag. "I'm starving."

With Ashford following, Cruz entered the kitchen and saw Madison shoving the last morsel of food into her mouth. "Maddie, I don't think you've been properly introduced to my friend." The girl spun on the stool, a ring of red sauce around her mouth. Cruz handed her a napkin and beckoned. "Wipe your mouth and hop down here."

Ashford chuckled at the sight. The pizza sauce on her face made her look like she had clown lips, thick and bright red.

When the child's face was clean and she had two feet on the floor, Cruz made introductions. "This is Madison." She extended her arm toward Ashford. "Maddie, I want you to meet Curtis Ashford. He's my friend. I call him, Ash."

Ashford knelt and crossed his forearms over his knee. "It's a pleasure to meet you, Madison."

The girl looked up at Cruz, who smiled and cocked her head toward her partner. "Say 'hello.'"

Madison faced Ashford and took a small step toward him. "Hello, Ash." The tiniest hint of a speech impediment made the word 'Ash' sound like 'ass.'

Cruz glanced at Ashford and took a knee behind

Madison. "Sweetheart, maybe it's better if you called—"

Ashford stopped her with a wave of his hand. "That's okay, Cruz. I've been called worse. Anyway, it sounds cute coming from her lips." He opened the bag. "I brought you some things, Madison." He pulled out items. "You've got some fresh pajamas in here...books...your video game you like—"

"Froggy," screamed Madison, sticking her hands into the bag and withdrawing a tattered green frog. "You brought Froggy." She hugged the stuffed animal and twisted her body back and forth. Without hesitation, she charged Ashford and threw her arms around his neck.

Ashford's body went rigid, his arms out at his sides. His eyes went to Cruz. She was smiling and making a hugging motion with her arms. He closed his arms around the girl and his large frame swallowed her. From behind, he appeared to be hugging himself.

Grinning, Cruz took her seat at the island and slapped a piece of pizza on a plate for Ashford. "Food's getting cold. Do you want another slice, Maddie?"

7:57 P.M.

After dinner, Special Agent Cruz cleaned the kitchen, while Ashford and Madison played in the living room. Above the noise of plates and forks clanging together, she heard him making goofy sounds, pretending to be some fantasy character, while Madison laughed, giggled and let out a periodic squeal. With him occupying the girl's attention, Cruz had taken the opportunity to sneak upstairs, use the facilities, get in a quick shower and change into a black tank top and a pair of black satin shorts.

As an FBI agent, she was usually dressed in a jacket and pants every day. She hated covering her legs. When she was on her own time, however, she wore shorts, skirts and dresses. It made no difference if the outside temperature was ten below or ninety-five. When she was home, the pants came off and she reached for shorter articles of clothing.

At seven thirty, after Ashford had left, she and Madison resumed their spots on the couch to finish watching the movie they had started.

Madison yawned, retracted her hand from under the blanket and plopped it into the bowl of popcorn resting on the couch. She stuffed the popcorn into her mouth and returned her hand to its original position, resting on Cruz's leg. Moments later, she slid her hand up and down the woman's leg. Cranking her head backward, she looked at Cruz upside down. "Your legs are smooth."

Cruz chuckled. "Well, thank you."

Madison went back to the television. "My Mommy has smooth legs."

Has. Noticing the present tense, Cruz held her breath.

"She has pretty long hair like yours, too."

Cruz bit her lower lip and swallowed.

"It's not as dark as yours." Madison yawned.

The day's events, which had been concealed for the last few hours with playing, laughter and good food, rushed to the forefront of Cruz's mind. She drove back the thoughts, but each time they returned with greater intensity. Eventually, Madison would have to confront the reality of her parent's fate. Cruz hoped and prayed that when the time came, the girl would have the support of family to comfort her and help her cope. Today, however, was not the time. Right now, she needed fun, a diversion from the truth, like the fun she had at the park.

Cruz averted her gaze. Her chin dropped to her chest. She had relished spending time with this little angel. Playing with Madison, seeing her smile—Cruz grinned— hearing her say Ashford's name had brought back dreams, dreams of having a child one day. The smile disappeared. Her joy had come at the cost of a double murder. Her chest tightened and she drew a deep breath, exhaling slowly. A shriek disrupted her guilt trip.

"Oh, no," screamed the girl when the television screen turned black.

Cruz punched buttons on the remote. Every channel displayed the same black screen. "I think we just lost our cable, Maddie." She tried a few more stations before hitting the power button and tossing the remote.

"What do we do now?"

Cruz saw the devastation in the girl's eyes, even though this was probably the tenth time she had seen the movie. "Well, it's getting late and I think you should be getting to bed."

Hearing those words, Madison's body went limp and she dropped her head onto Cruz's lap. There were no tears, only a melodramatic display of displeasure.

Unable to resist, Cruz started a tickle fight that concluded with the two of them rolling onto the floor with wide grins and rosy cheeks, gasping for air. "All right, I'll tell you what. You head upstairs and get ready for bed and I'll be up to read you a bedtime story. How's that sound?"

Madison jumped to her feet and bolted for the stairs.

"Use the bathroom," a ringing sound came from the kitchen, "in my bedroom. I set out a toothbrush for you. It's on the sink." She hurried into the kitchen and snatched her phone. "Hey, Jack. What's up?"

Jack Johnson, an ex-Marine in his sixties, was her

next-door neighbor. His wife had passed away a few years ago. Being retired and living alone, he had extra time on his hands. When he could, he helped Cruz with some of the manual labor around her house, cutting the lawn, removing snow from the driveway, raking leaves. He was a good man and the two of them had hit it off the first day she moved into the house.

"Hi, Raychel, I'm good. I'm sorry to call so late, but I'm heading out in the morning and I was hoping you could keep an eye on the place, pick up the mail and newspaper. I should only be gone for a few days...going to see the grandkids."

"Of course," she replied, flashing her eyes upstairs when she heard water running.

"Thanks. I appreciate it." He paused. "So, I see you're entertaining tonight."

"Yeah, it's a long story." She heard papers ruffling through the phone.

"I happened to be looking out the window when you got home this afternoon."

Madison yelled from the top of the stairs. "Raychel, I'm all ready for bed."

Jack spoke at the same time. "She looks cute as a bug."

"Okay, Sweetie. Get in bed and I'll be right up." Cruz watched the girl skip down the hall before concurring with her neighbor, "Yes, she certainly is."

"Is she your niece?"

"I can't get into it. I'm working a case and—" She paused. "All I can say is she'll be spending the night."

"I get it. You don't have to explain. If you need anything, don't hesitate to call."

"Thanks, Jack. Don't worry about your place. I'll get the mail and paper. Have a safe trip." She started to pull away the phone, but stopped. "Hey, did your cable go out?"

"Yeah, about ten minutes ago. I called the company. Apparently, the whole neighborhood is down. They said they'd have someone out here within the hour."

"Thanks, Jack. That saves me a phone call. Good night."

Jack bid Cruz farewell and disconnected the call.

. . .

"And, the king said, 'Wherever you go, my love will always be there with you.'" Cruz closed the book and said, "The end." She stood. "The end, and it's time to say your prayers and get to bed."

"I don't say prayers."

"Why not?" said Cruz, tilting her head.

Madison shrugged. "I don't know. I just don't."

Cruz rolled her hand toward her chest, beckoning her guest to join her. "Well, tonight you're in for a treat, because you and I are going to say our prayers together." She went to her knees, put her elbows on the bed and folded her hands. "Just do what I do and repeat after me." When Madison was kneeling beside her, Cruz touched her hand to her forehead. The doorbell rang. "You stay put and I'll be right back." She grabbed a wine-colored knee-length satin robe from her bedroom and slid her arms into the sleeves.

Standing at the front door, she peeked through the peephole. A man in a light blue striped shirt and baseball cap stood at the door, clipboard in his hands. She remembered her conversation with Jack. *He must be with the cable company.* A quick look at his uniform confirmed her assumption. She opened the door.

"Good evening, ma'am. I'm sorry for disturbing you. I'm with the cable company and I need to check your router. The whole neighborhood is out and I need to verify your settings to make sure the signal doesn't go out again after I'm gone. It should only take five minutes."

Cruz escorted him to the living room and pointed out the location of the router.

"Thank you. I'll only be a few minutes, ten at the most."

"I'll be upstairs if you need me. Just holler."

Once upstairs, she knelt beside Madison. Touching the fingers of her right hand to her forehead, chest, left and right shoulder, she said, "In the name of the Father and of the Son and of the Holy Spirit." She watched the girl copy her movements. Wanting to keep the prayers simple, she opted to pray the Our Father. "Our Father, Who art in Heaven..." Two minutes later, she finished, saying, "Deliver us from evil. Amen."

Putting extra emphasis on the word, Madison said, "Amen."

"We finish by making the sign of the cross again." Cruz touched her forehead. Hearing a man's voice at the bottom of the stairs, she pivoted her head toward the source.

"Excuse me, ma'am, but I need you to come down here for a moment. I've found a problem."

"Okay, I'll be right there." She spun back toward Madison. "We'll finish—" Cruz put her hand on the girl's shoulder, "What is it, Sweetie? What's wrong?" The girl was shaking uncontrollably, her chin and lips trembling. There was a dark spot above the crotch of her pajamas, growing larger by the second. Moments later, Cruz whipped her head back and forth from the doorway to Madison. Her heart rate doubled and her adrenaline spiked.

The muscles in Special Agent Cruz's stomach convulsed. She hopped to her feet and steered Madison toward the closet, whispering to the girl, "You stay in here and be really, really quiet. Don't come out, until I say so...okay?" Cruz could not tell if she understood. The terrified blank stare said more than any words could say. She was in shock.

"Ma'am," said the man's voice.

Cruz's back stiffened. The voice was closer. He was coming up the stairs. She heard a board creak. Only two steps made a noise. Each one had a unique sound. He was three steps from the second floor. She eased the closet door shut and spun around, her eyes scanning the room for a weapon. Her service pistol was in the safe, under her bed. Out of her routine, she had forgotten to grab her Ruger LC9s, a smaller and lighter pistol she carried around the house. She spotted an extension pole for a duster in the corner. Darting across the room, she loosened, extended and twisted the pole to create a longer stick. Wrapping her hands around the handle, she took a half swing. Out of options and out of time, the pole would have to suffice.

"Ma'am, it's me. Are you up here? You need to have a look at this."

Cruz heard the tone in his voice. He was no longer a

'cable guy.' He was a killer. She took a position next to the open door, back to the wall, and raised her weapon. With the element of surprise, she had one shot at this. Lifting the pole, she made a few quick and short strikes, her mind judging the distance to the opposite side of the doorway. If she struck the doorjamb, instead of him, it was game over. Staring at the carpeting outside the room, she looked like a baseball player getting ready for the pitch. Shifting her weight back and forth from one bare foot to the other, she wagged the pole.

. . .

The man stopped talking and inched further down the hallway, slowly placing one foot in front of the other. He sensed his ruse was not working. His target was an FBI agent after all. It was her job to sense things, know when someone was lying. There was one thing left to do—find the woman and the kid and put bullets into them. He stopped at the first bedroom, the one from which the woman's voice had originated. His ear straining, he heard nothing, but he felt her presence. She was in there. He took a deep, silent breath. She was near. Her perfume spoke when she chose not to speak. Grasping tighter the butt of his silenced twenty-two caliber pistol, he faced the doorway and edged his body further down the hallway, pointing the pistol toward the bedroom. The furniture slowly became visible—bed with ruffled blankets. Two steps more and the closet came into view. His body was half exposed. His left foot took another step and his eye caught a shadow flash across the upper part of the left wall.

. . .

Motionless, Cruz waited, her eyes fixed on the carpeting. The black silhouette on the shag fibers got bigger and bigger. She squeezed her hands. *Come on...just a little more.* The shadow grew and she jumped into action. Dropping to her right knee, she leaned in the same direction and acquired her target. She swung the pole at an upward angle and made contact with the pistol and the man's fingers. He let out a yell and recoiled, taking a step backward. The pistol fell from his hand, landing a foot away from him. Cruz was three times farther away from the weapon. If he got to the gun first, she and Madison were dead. She peered into his cold, dark, emotionless eyes. He stopped rubbing his hand and snarled. He was thinking the same thing.

Cruz lunged forward and flopped to her stomach, extending the pole; the end hit the top of the gun's slide. The force of her strike sent the pistol sliding across the hall, under the handrail and down to the main floor. The playing field was a bit more level. With both hands on the pole, she whipped it upward, smacking the man between his legs. He clutched his groin and his legs wobbled before he dropped to his knees.

Cruz sprang to her feet and thrust the pole at the man's head. He dodged the assault, grabbed the pole and spun her around, until her back hit the handrail. Her eyes glanced to the right. The first floor was a long way down. With each of them grasping the pole with both hands, the man pushed; however, still on his knees, he could not generate enough power to send her over the handrail. Cruz pushed back and mounted a counter assault. She lifted her right leg and drove her foot into his chest, while yanking on the pole. He released his hold, did a reverse somersault and got to his feet in one fluid motion. Favoring his smarting testicles with one hand, he retrieved a knife from his pocket with the other hand. His thumb moved forward and a double-edged blade shot out from the handle, accompanied by the sound of steel grinding against steel.

Ten feet away and facing him, Cruz took a step backward and broke the pole over her knee, leaving her with two shorter sticks. She assumed a fighting stance and zeroed in on her adversary. He sneered.

Closing the distance between him and Cruz, he growled, "I'm going to carve you up." He swung the knife left and right, while advancing. She backpedaled and timed his swings. He swiped the blade to his right, opening his body. She strode headlong, swinging the sticks in front of her body. The right one hit his weapon hand. The left one struck the right side of his face, his head rotating with the blow. She kicked him in the groin and recovered her balance before raising her foot and connecting with his chest. He stumbled backwards and latched on to the handrail to keep his body righted. She marched down the hall, the sticks slicing through the air, sounding like tiny helicopter blades. Two whacks to the head, one on each side of his face, and he stood straighter. Blinking, he whipped his head left and right, trying to maintain consciousness. Cruz had him on the ropes and she knew it. A couple more strikes and he was going down.

He knew it, too. Lowering his head, he charged, getting his body between her outstretched arms, more importantly, the weapons in her hands. Grabbing a handful of the right sleeve of her robe, he tossed the knife a short ways into the air. Acquiring a hammer grip, he raised his arm.

Cruz saw the overhand strike coming. Letting go of the right stick, she spun her body to the left and slipped her right arm out of robe, narrowly missing the blade as it ripped the garment in half. Her attacker threw aside his half of the fabric and lumbered toward her. Removing the other half of her robe, she transferred her weapon and wrapped the clothing around her left hand. The satin material afforded little, if any, protection from the blade of the knife. She studied her approaching opponent, noting his glistening eyes in the dim beam of the overhead light. He had not recovered from the wallops to his skull. She bided her time, waiting for him to start the overhand strike. The man took another awkward step, paused and blinked a few times. His body swayed slightly before his weapon hand moved upward.

Cruz struck.

Lowering her body, she raced under the man's raised arm. Circling behind him, she delivered several cracks to the back of his head, following up with brutal punches to his kidneys. She looked like a boxer working out on a heavy bag. Bellowing, he arched his back and looked to the ceiling before spinning to his right and wildly slicing at the air. She ducked under the feeble attempt. His momentum sent him floundering toward the handrail. Drawing back her right arm, she let it fly. The stick caught him on the right side of the neck. The man's body went limp and listed toward the handrail. His above average height worked to his disadvantage. The assassin's thighs met the handrail and his body folded in half. For a moment, it seemed as if he was stuck. A split-second later, his legs toppled over the handrail and he disappeared.

After she heard a heavy thud and the sound of breaking glass, Cruz leaned on the handrail and looked down. His body lay near the couch, which had been rotated forty-five degrees. His arms and legs were crumpled and bent at awkward angles. His head was cocked abnormally far to one side and his body was still. Gasping for air, Cruz lowered her head. *Thank you...Lord, for the...strength...*

Before she could finish the prayer, the front door opened and a man dressed similar to her deceased attacker appeared. She lifted her head and their eyes met.

Glimpsing his partner, he fixed her with a cold, hard glare.

Special Agent Cruz had seconds before the second man would be up the stairs and closing in on her. Just like the first, the second assassin would have a gun. She sprinted down the hall. Extending her arms, she slammed into the doorjamb of her bedroom, changed course and ran toward the bed. Throwing her feet forward, she slid on her hip and knee. Her hands shot under the bed and pulled out a gun safe. Punching in the four-digit code, the door popped open and she clamped her fingers around the Glock 23 and darted back to the doorway. Staying back from the doorjamb, she leaned to the right, pistol forward. The man was at the top of the staircase. She fired several rounds and watched him dive to the floor. On his back, he pointed his weapon at her. She saw tiny flashes. The sound of the bullets hitting the bathroom door behind her was louder than the report from the silenced twenty-two. She ducked into the bedroom.

Dropping to one knee, she leaned out again. He was gone. *Did he leave? Is he hiding?* A second later, Cruz had her answer when the wallboard in front of her face came apart. Jerking her body behind cover, she caught a glimpse of the assailant. He was in the first bedroom opposite the staircase. Madison's room was between them. Getting to her feet, she bobbed her head out and back. It was clear. Whipping her firearm into the hallway, she waited, her finger applying steady pressure to the trigger. *Wait for him, Raychel.* Her eyes moved up and down. She was anticipating where he would expose himself—high or low. The gun's muzzle followed her eyes. *He was high last time.* Cruz lowered the muzzle and guessed wrong. She recovered in time to see him poke his head out at the same spot. They fired in unison, their rounds zipping parallel to the wall. The blast from her Glock overpowered the muffled pops from the man's twenty-two. Pieces of wallboard slapped her forehead and she whirled back into the bedroom.

Studying the pistol, Cruz's eyebrows dipped and her lips disappeared into her mouth. If her math was correct, she had three rounds left. Her eyes shifted toward the closet. Shooting a quick glance toward the hallway, she shoved her body away from the wall and ran across the room, stealing a glimpse over her shoulder. She threw open the door and stepped inside the closet. Her fingers tapped buttons on a keypad. A metal latch, securing a Mossberg 500 shotgun to the wall, released. Cruz racked the gun, while darting back to the doorway. The shotgun's stock had an ammunition sleeve that held six, twelve gauge rounds. She plucked one of the shells and shoved it into the magazine tube before bringing the weapon to her shoulder. With her back to the wall, she looked upward and pointed the barrel in the same direction. She opened her mouth. Her lips puckering, she let out a quick breath and steeled herself for the deafening roar and body-battering recoil that was to come.

Formulating a plan, Cruz's mind drifted to Madison. The death of the girl's parents had been traumatic. If that nightmare were not enough to ensure the need for counseling, these unfolding events would. She shook her head and pressed the shotgun to her shoulder. *First things first.* She had to save Madison's life. Nothing else mattered.

Cruz swung the long gun out, her body following. She crept down the hall in a low crouch to make herself a smaller target. As a bonus, the lower center of gravity would help control the recoil. She made her way to Madison's room and glanced left. The closet door was closed. *Good girl, Maddie...Stay put.* Shifting her gaze to the right and peering through the slats in the handrail, she saw the top of a man's head at the bottom of the staircase. *Crap...a third one!* She tightened her grip on the shotgun. *All right, there's plenty for everyone. Come and get it.*

Before she had taken another step, three booms from the first floor echoed off every hard surface in the house. She hefted the Mossberg over the handrail and stared at the gunman over the smooth barrel. Standing in a Weaver stance at the base of the stairs and pointing his Colt 1911 at the upstairs bedroom, where the second attacker was holed up, was her neighbor. She directed the muzzle of her weapon at the same bedroom doorway. Her mouth pressed against the wooden stock, her words came out muffled. "I can't tell you how good it is to see you, Jack."

"I heard the roar of your forty-cal and took off running."

Bless you, Jack, Cruz thought.

"I winged him, but I don't think he's out of the fight. Watch yourself."

Cruz heard a scratching sound coming from the bedroom. She put more pressure on the trigger and held her breath. The scratching sound intensified before the torso of a man appeared, pointing toward two o'clock.

Cruz shouted, "Freeze...Don't move or I'll..." her voice trailed off, as the man crashed to the floor, "shoot." The man's eyes were open, but lifeless.

"Talk to me, Raychel." Jack was standing on the third step. "What's going on? Is he down?"

She approached the man and kicked the twenty-two out of his hand. A minute passed and his eyes had not moved. "The second floor's clear, Jack. We're good up here."

"Stay there." Jack reversed course. "I'll clear the main floor."

After verifying the assassin was dead, she made a beeline for Madison.

March 21st, 8:05 a.m.
J. Edgar Hoover Building
Washington, D.C.

Ashford pushed the chair away from the conference table in Special Agent Cruz's office and sat cross-legged, his ankle resting on his knee. Glancing up, he stared out the window on the other side of the table. Twenty-four hours earlier, the sun had been shining and people had on shorts. Today, you were nuts if you left the house without a winter jacket. The temperature had dropped more than forty degrees ahead of a cold front, ushering in a late-season storm of mixed precipitation. He watched people walking bent over to keep from being blown backward by sustained wind speeds of 35 miles per hour, gusting to 50 miles per hour. Out of the corner of his eye, he saw Cruz yawning, while she flipped through the report he had given her. "Did you get much sleep last night?"

"Hmm..." She let go of the last page of the report. Tilting her head backward, she rubbed her eyes with the heel of her palms. "Oh, I..." Stretching her arms above her head, her reply came through another yawn. "I got...a couple...of hours." Opening her eyes, she gazed out the window and reflected on what had happened after Jack cleared the main floor of her house.

Cruz never left Madison's side, while the police and FBI agents secured the crime scene and removed the bodies of the killers. She read books to the girl, played video games and taught her how to play 'Rock/Paper/Scissors.' At two in the morning, Madison fell asleep. For half an hour, Cruz held her and watched her sleep, until she could no longer keep her eyes open. She was awakened at 3 a.m. when Ashford touched her shoulder and told her Madison's grandparents were waiting downstairs. She had tried to convince them to let the girl sleep until morning, but they wanted her away from the macabre landscape. Cruz could not blame them. She would have wanted the same thing. While her intentions had been noble, she realized a part of her was not ready to see her new friend leave.

Cruz was successful, however, in encouraging the grandparents to seek protective custody for them and Madison, until all perpetrators in the investigation were brought to justice. The attack on her house five hours after she assumed guardianship of Madison was no coincidence. Cruz was convinced the men were there to kill the girl.

After setting up the protection detail and accompanying the trio to the safe house, Cruz went to Jack's house and slept on the living room couch. He had insisted she stay away from her place, until the FBI crime lab had gathered evidence and a restoration company had cleaned the house. He also persisted on being the one who would make the phone calls and oversee the cleanup process. Cruz was too tired to fight him on both counts. She thanked him and fell asleep on the couch.

Cruz faced Ashford. He was staring and smiling at her. "What is it?"

"You didn't hear a word I said, did you?"

She raised her eyebrows and rolled her eyes to the ceiling. She nodded. "I said I got a few hours of sleep."

Chuckling, he uncrossed his legs and leaned forward. "I said 'why don't you get some more Z's and I'll visit Payne Laboratories?' You—"

She shook her head and shot down his offer. "Not a chance, Ash. I'll be fine."

He pulled away. Her tone was cutting, but he dismissed it. She was beat and not her usual self.

Cruz tapped the papers on the table. "So, we've got two professional hitters with a military background."

Ashford had gotten the early reports from the FBI crime lab. The two men who broke into her house were in their late twenties and had served almost ten years in the Army. Their history after that was spotty. They had never filed tax returns and did not have a place of residence. They were not ghosts, but they had maintained a low profile and a thin digital footprint. The initial information suggested they worked illegal jobs for cash and moved around a lot.

"It looks that way. Ballistics will be able to tell us if

the same guns were used to kill the Wilson's, but we won't have that report until later in the day. My money's on a match."

Cruz agreed. "But, what is so important about Jason and Jane Wilson that contract killers were sent to their home?"

Ashford checked his watch. "Well, that's question number one for Mr. Payne." He and Cruz had a nine o'clock meeting with the CEO. He stood and plucked his jacket from the chair. "We better get going if we want to be on time. Traffic is going to be nasty."

9:32 A.M.
RESTON, VIRGINIA
PAYNE LABORATORIES

The red-haired secretary sat behind a much too long counter/desk smiled, her plump cheeks pushing up the oval eyeglasses resting on her sloped nose. "Mr. Payne will be with you shortly, sir." Her figure was chunky, but the black form-fitting business suit clung to her voluptuous body, conferring on her the hint of the hourglass shape most women sought. Ashford spied the loosely tied ball of hair at the back of her head and he envisioned the attractive woman with her hair down. He fought to keep his tone even. "That's what you've been saying for the last half hour..." he read her nametag, "Ms. Patrick." He forced a smile that shown as a grimace. "You should try mixing up your answers." He spun around before she had a chance to respond.

As soon as Ashford lowered his frame into the chair next to his partner, Cruz jumped up. "That's it. I'm done." She bolted for the door with the name 'Henry Payne, President & CEO' on it, catching the attention of his gatekeeper.

Ms. Patrick stood as quickly as Cruz did, sending her chair rolling away from the station. She met the FBI agent at the office door. "Ma'am, you can't go in there. Mr. Payne is meeting with a client." She reached for Cruz's hand.

Grasping the doorknob, Cruz glared at the younger woman out of her half-shut left eye. "Watch me."

The woman halted her forward progress and retracted her hand.

. . .

Henry Payne threw his head back and roared with laughter. He took a few seconds to quiet himself. He regarded his friend seated across from the desk. "Those were good times, William."

William replied, "We should get the boys together and take a couple of days to revisit those good times...maybe this weekend."

"I can't. I'm afraid I'm up to here," he placed his open hand under his chin, "with work."

"You work too hard. You need to—" William stopped speaking when the door flew open behind him.

Hearing his assistant's agitated voice, the smile on Payne's face disappeared.

"Ma'am, please, this meeting is very important."

Cruz burst into the room. Catching Payne's attention, she spoke to both the woman behind her and the man in front of her. Her voice was sharp. "A murder investigation is important, too." With one hand on the doorknob and her weight shifted to one foot, she used the other hand to draw back the lapel of her dress jacket—revealing her badge—before resting the hand on the waistband of her navy blue slacks. Coupled with the boisterous intrusion, the move was a power play to regain the upper hand, having waited on Payne for more than thirty minutes.

The woman brushed by Cruz. "I'm sorry, sir. She just—"

Payne held up his hand. "That's all right, Ms. Patrick." He stood, buttoned his suit coat and walked around his desk. Smiling, he shook hands with his friend and extended his arm toward the door. "Thank you for meeting with me this morning, William. It's been good seeing you again. I'll look everything over and get back with you in a couple days."

Her eyes never leaving Payne's face, Cruz sidestepped to allow the shorter man to leave. She felt Ashford's presence off her left shoulder.

Payne strode toward his guests. A broad smile on his face, he addressed them. "You must be Agent's DelaCruz and Ashford from the FBI." He stuck out his hand. "I'm very sorry for keeping you waiting. A man in my position tries desperately to keep a tight schedule, but sometimes things don't go according to plan. Please accept my apologies."

She let his hand hover in the air for a few moments—another power move. Shaking his hand, she examined his features. Payne was easily six-feet, two-inches tall and had a lanky frame. With a full head of white hair, coupled with light blue eyes and one of the most charming smiles she had ever seen, he was an attractive man for his advanced years, which she guessed to be in the sixties. Releasing her grip, she glanced at his hand. *Soft hands...I'll bet they don't do their own dirty work.* Having struck a harsh tone, she dialed down her demeanor. "Thank you for agreeing to see us on such short notice."

He motioned toward the two chairs facing his desk. "Please, sit down."

Cruz and Ashford followed the man. She pivoted her head left and right. Payne had good taste. Mahogany-paneled walls complemented the ornate furniture, including the lavish eight-foot Victorian double pedestal executive desk with an inlaid faded red leather surface. Her eyes went to the floor when her chunky one-inch high heels landed on a Persian hand knotted area rug. Guessing the masterpiece cost more than her car, she speculated what the toll charge would be for crossing.

Payne unbuttoned his suit coat. "So, what can I do for you? Can I get either of you a cup of coffee? I can have Greta bring you anything you like—latte, cappuccino, straight-up cup of Joe." He sat and rested his hand on the desk phone.

Cruz shook her head one time. "No, we're good."

"All right then." He reclined, resting his elbows on the armrests and touching his fingertips together. "What's this all about?" He rotated his wrist to view his watch. "I don't mean to rush you, but I do have a ten o'clock."

"I'm sure they won't mind waiting. You have a nice waiting area." She gestured toward the antique grandfather clock in the corner. "We've been looking at it for the last *forty* minutes."

He smiled and tipped his head. "As I said..."

She adjusted her position in the chair. "Mr. Payne, what can you tell us about a couple of your employees—Jason and Jane Wilson?" To her right, she saw Ashford cross his legs after sitting.

Payne shrugged. "They're two of my best employees...brilliant minds, very nice people. Their work helped launch three drugs that fight high blood pressure and artery disease." He leaned forward. "I hope they're not in trouble."

Cruz glanced at Ashford. "They're dead...murdered in their home night before last."

Payne's mouth fell open. "That's terrible." He rocked backward, exhaling. "I must apologize again, Agent DelaCruz. If I'd had known I would've postponed my meeting with William and seen you right away. How can I help?"

"You can start by telling us about their work. What projects were they working on? Did they have any conflicts with fellow employees? Were any threats made against them?"

Payne's gaze vacillated between the agents. He

cleared his throat. "I can tell you that neither of them had any problems with their co-workers. They were nice folks, who got along with everyone. As for the projects they were working on...I'm afraid I can't discuss that with you. I'm sure—"

"You can't or you won't," Cruz shot back.

His face tightened and he flexed his jaw muscles. "I'm sure you can understand the nature of our industry. It takes years, and costs millions, to create and test a new drug." He shrugged and lifted his open hands into the air. "Even then, it may not meet FDA approval and we lose. My point is...secrecy is paramount in this business. After spending that much time and money, we don't want a rival company stealing our research and beating us to market." He chuckled. "If that happened, we wouldn't stay in business very long."

Cruz crossed her legs. "I would think you'd want to know who killed your employees and why they were killed."

"I do. I'm just not willing to give away trade secrets in the process." He paused. "Do you have any suspects?"

"We've already caught the men who killed the Wilsons."

Payne scratched his temple. "I'm sorry. You said you've already caught the men who did this. Then, why are you here?"

"The same guys who murdered Jason and Jane Wilson broke into my house last night and tried to kill me."

Ashford shot a quick look at his partner. They were waiting on the ballistics report to confirm their suspicions. She was using the information to elicit a reaction from the CEO and impress upon him the importance of his full cooperation.

Payne jerked his head back.

Her hands resting on the chair's armrests, she lifted her thumb toward her chest. "I'm still here. *They're* not with us anymore." She let her words hang in the air. His arched eyebrows told her he got the implication.

"I'm glad you're okay, Agent DelaCruz; however, that doesn't answer my question. If those responsible for the Wilson's murder have," he hesitated before choosing his words, "been dealt with, then why are you here? I fail to see how this affects me?"

"We got the trigger men, but those who ordered the hit are still out there."

Payne brought his eyebrows together. "You think this was some...murder for hire?"

"I can't get into the specifics of the case, but yes. That's why we need to know the nature of the Wilson's work. We need to find out *why* they were killed." She rubbed her thumb and forefinger together. "Someone with deep pockets wanted them dead. The same someone was also willing to invade an FBI agent's house and attempt to eliminate the Wilson's daughter, presumably to keep her from identifying the assassins. Tying up loose ends, you could say. What were the Wilsons working on,

Mr. Payne?"

"I've already told you—"

"Yes, I know. You can't discuss that with us." Cruz clenched the armrests of the chair and shoved herself to her feet. "I can get a search warrant and order you to turn over every last scrap of information. I can tie up your operations for days, weeks...maybe even months. Who knows how long this investigation will take?" She leaned into him. "I can play hardball, too."

Payne squinted, his nostrils flaring. "I'm sure you can, Agent DelaCruz." He stood. Towering over her, he fixed her with a hard glare. "This is the big leagues, however. If you come after me," he twirled his finger at Cruz's groin, "you better make damn sure you leave behind your lace panties and put on a pair of *big boy* pants. I have powerful connections."

Ashford took a step toward Payne. "You smug son of—"

Cruz planted her hand on Ashford's chest and stared at Payne. His charming demeanor had evaporated, revealing a crass old man, who fell back on his power and wealth when threatened. "I can assure you my choice of undergarments will have no bearing on the execution of my duties. The second I was attacked and a little girl's life was at risk, this became *personal*. I won't rest until everyone involved is behind bars." She took an exaggerated look around the office. "Money and power won't matter when I find the man who sent hit men to my home."

Payne jutted his chin toward her, his chest inflated.

Cruz smiled and turned her back on the man. Halfway to the door, she called out to him over her shoulder. "Have a nice day, Mr. Payne. We'll be in touch."

Three steps outside of the office, Cruz looked at Ashford out of the corner of her eye. She kept her voice low. "I want a search warrant by noon. He's not going to stonewall me."

"I'll start with Judge Thompkins. He's always been good to us."

Cruz stopped at the elevator and tapped the down-arrow button. Spinning around, she saw Payne. He had his desk phone to his ear. For several seconds, the two stared at each other like kids waiting for the other to blink. Neither one wavered. The overhead chime and the opening of the elevator door forced Cruz to turn away.

Payne watched the Special Agent leave his line of sight. A female voice came over the phone.

"This is Senator's Payne's office."

"I need to speak with the Senator."

"I'm sorry, but Senator Payne is in a meeting at the moment. May I have—"

"I don't give a damn if he's in a meeting. This is—" He pinched the bridge of his nose and slammed shut his eyes, taking a second to quell his anger. "Tell him it's his brother. I need to speak with him, *immediately*."

"I'm sorry, sir—"

"I don't need you to apologize. I need you to get a message to your boss before I inform him about his *incompetent* secretary. Do I make myself clear?" Hearing silence, he raised his voice. "You're not very bright, are you, missy? I'll slow down for you. Get...my...brother...*now*."

The woman's voice cracking, she replied, "Yes, sir."

12:02 P.M.
BETHESDA, MARYLAND

Jaleo was a colorful tapas bar, focused on Spanish fare. The full-length glass windows on either side of the front door contributed to the establishment's light, airy and upscale feel. From any seat, customers had a view of the hustle and bustle taking place at the intersection of Woodmont Avenue and Elm Street. An outdoor seating area on the north side indulged those who wanted a closer connection to the street traffic. On this cold and windy day, however, the chairs and tables had been removed for fear they would be blown away. Besides, no one was interested in dining outdoors.

In the back of the restaurant, sitting in a half-round red booth with two blue straight-back chairs on the other side of a circular bistro table, Mitchell Dawson could see everyone approaching and entering from Elm Street. He had a clear view of the front door, able to see patrons before they could see him. Plus, in case of emergencies, an alternate exit was right behind his booth. In his line of work, one could never take too many precautions. A secondary escape door had saved his life more times than he could count.

Nursing his glass of Spanish Collins, a creation of Beefeater Gin, Manzanilla sherry and fresh lime juice, Dawson took a sip and returned the drink to the table.

"Your food will right out." The server gestured. "Can I get you another?"

Dawson eyed the tall and lean young woman. Her smiling bright red lips offset the jet-black color of her shoulder-length hair and full eyebrows. He dropped his gaze to her white blouse. The thread holding the black buttons was stretched to its limit. If she took a deep breath, everything underneath the shirt would be on display. Below the blouse, a black mini skirt showed most of her legs, which were covered with black fishnet pantyhose. With the perfect amount of makeup, she was an extremely striking woman. Her outfit was more befitting for a night out on the town than for the lunchtime crowd at a restaurant; however, he was confident her attire contributed to the generous tips she undoubtedly received from diners.

Dawson returned her smile. He guessed her to be in her early twenties, at least a dozen years younger than him. "Thank you..." he glanced at the nametag, strategically placed a little lower on her chest and waved his hand above his glass, "Estelle. I'm good for now."

"I'll be back in a few minutes with your sandwich." She whirled around and headed toward another table.

Dawson gawked at her, starting at the long and shapely legs and finishing at the smooth dark hair, glimmering when the overhead lights shone on it at the right angle. This was not the first time Estelle had waited on him. The two had a history, a financial history. He had always tipped her very well, planning to get a little extra for his money one day. He grinned. *Women aren't the only ones who can play hard to get.*

Dawson checked his watch. The man he was meeting was late. Tardiness was a common tactic used by those who knew they were outmatched. They felt the technique gave them the upper hand during negotiations. Ironically, showing up late made them appear weak in the eyes of their adversary. No, the only thing that afforded a person power was power. The projection of strength was what everyone respected. He tipped back his glass and caught sight of his man, jogging across Elm Street, holding out his hand to stop a car.

Entering the restaurant, the man's eyes and head darted left and right, while he brushed the snow from his overcoat. He waved off a host and started moving to his left. Navigating between the tables, he spotted Dawson and picked up his pace before coming to a quick stop, dragging out one of the chairs and plopping into it. He set his briefcase on the floor and sighed. "I'm sorry I'm late. Traffic was horrendous." He unbuttoned his coat, but did not remove it. "So, what's so important that we had to meet in the middle of the day?"

Dawson saw Estelle bringing his food, a grilled Manchego, Valdeón and goat cheese sandwich with truffle oil on rustic bread. After she had taken the new arrival's order and left, Dawson unfolded a napkin and laid it on his lap. He took a big bite and closed his eyes, his taste buds savoring the flavor of the combination of cheeses. Swallowing, he saw his contact staring at him.

"A grilled cheese and wine?" said the man. "An odd choice if you ask me."

Dawson put the sandwich on his plate and reached for the napkin. "I'm *not* asking you, Charles."

Using his forefinger, Charles Patterson pushed his wire-rimmed eyeglasses further up the bridge of his nose. He combed his dark hair with his fingers before taking off his overcoat and straightening the navy blue tie beneath his black suit coat.

Watching Patterson primp, Dawson poked his tongue lightly into his cheek and inhaled deeply. The twenty-something graduate of Harvard had an irritating air about him. Fortunately, the money for this job was good, more than compensating for having to interact with this twitchy, arrogant little man. Not hungry anymore, he pushed his plate away and rested his elbows on the table, interlocking his fingers and raising his hands to his mouth. "We've hit a snag. The girl is still alive and I need *you* to find out where the FBI has taken her."

Patterson whipped his head around, checking to see if anyone was listening.

Behind his clasped hands, Dawson smirked at the man's pathetic attempt to demonstrate his knowledge of the spy game.

"You were paid to *take out* all of them. First, your men screw up at the house and let the girl slip through their fingers. Now you're telling me the girl is still alive. What happened?"

Dawson felt his face getting warm. He was not accustomed to taking orders, especially from people like Patterson. "I dispatched my men to the FBI Agent's house last night. When they didn't check in on time, I did some investigating. There were a fleet of federal vehicles in the agent's driveway and lining the street. Two body bags were brought out and I caught a glimpse of the female agent."

Patterson leaned in and lowered his voice. "They're *both* alive?" He exhaled and rolled his head. "I'm beginning to think we're paying you too much. We could've hired a couple of street thugs for a lot less if we wanted a mess on our hands."

Dawson clamped his jaw shut and spoke through gritted teeth. "Listen to me, you half-witted twit. I *may* tolerate that kind of attitude from your boss, but certainly not from *you*. Keep it up and you won't live to regret it."

Patterson opened his mouth to speak, but held his tongue when he spotted the man across from him clutching a table knife and glaring at him.

Dawson jabbed the knife at the air separating the two men. "This woman killed two of my men. I'll take care of *her. You* need to focus on getting me the whereabouts of the girl. Got it?"

"Wait a minute." Patterson leaned backward and glanced off into the distance. "So, the men you sent to do the job are dead?" He held his arms out at his sides, palms up. "That's great. Even if the girl *can* identify your people, there's nothing leading them back to my employer. Dead men don't speak." He dismissed Dawson with a wave of his hand. "Forget about the girl and the agent. They can't hurt us anymore."

Dawson grabbed the sleeve of Patterson's suit coat and jerked the man closer, while getting in his face. He kept his voice low, so no one could hear him, but the man inches away. "I lost two of my best men. I wouldn't call that *great.*" He spied the other patrons. It took everything in his power to keep from jamming the dull knife into this man's skinny neck. "Besides, I have a reputation to uphold. When I take a job, I *finish* it. This isn't just about you and your boss anymore. Find the girl."

Beads of perspiration formed on Patterson's forehead and he swallowed hard. "And, what if I don't?" His pulse pounded in his head.

Dawson let go of the man's suit coat, worked his way to the end of the booth and stood. Fishing out enough money from his wallet to pay the check and give Estelle a substantial gratuity, he tossed the bills onto the table. "You're a smart Ivy-Leaguer, Charles. I'm sure you can figure out what'll happen if I don't get my way." He slapped Patterson on the back and strolled out of the restaurant.

1:09 P.M.
WASHINGTON, D.C.

Judging from the scowl on her partner's face and the way he was rubbing the back of his neck, Special Agent Cruz knew he had bad news to share. "Don't tell me."

Shaking his head, Ashford shuffled toward her desk and fell back into one of two chairs facing her. He expanded his chest and let it fall, expelling a noisy breath through his mouth.

"That's the fourth judge to turn us down."

"They all say the same thing, Cruz. There's not enough evidence to justify a search warrant." He shrugged. "We need more."

She threw her body backward into her chair and held out her arms toward Ashford, showing him her palms. "And, how do we get that evidence if we're not allowed to *dig* for it?" She tossed her pen onto the desk and massaged her temples with her thumbs.

Since leaving Payne Laboratories, Ashford had contacted four judges to obtain a search warrant for Payne Laboratories—no success. In between phone calls, he had reviewed everything available on the Wilsons—

financial statements, phone records, criminal history, Facebook and Twitter accounts. On paper, they were a typical American couple with jobs and bills to pay. Nothing about them justified a professional hit.

Cruz had worked her military contacts to get more information on the two assassins. Compiling a list of men who had served with the killers, she tried to find a connection the two might have had with a third party. These men did not work alone. Someone above them had to be giving the orders and assigning the jobs. After contacting several of the ex-servicemen on the list, she was no further ahead in finding the killer's boss.

Ashford jutted his chin toward the papers on her desk. "Any luck?"

She picked up a sheet of paper and looked at the one beneath it. "I think we're going to have to get out there and knock on some doors if we want answers. These guys are tight-lipped when it comes to their fellow soldiers. We need to stress the importance of any help they can provide. For that...a face-to-face is needed." Her head shot up. "What about the ballistics report?"

Ashford snapped his fingers. "That's the other thing...it's just as we thought. The report confirms that both shooters were involved in the Wilson's murder as well as the attack on you and Madison."

"I guess that's good news, even though we already knew it. At least, we can stop speculating now." Cruz cranked her head and stared out the window. She had done everything possible from her office. Unable to get the search warrant, she was contemplating going back to Payne Laboratories and eating crow. If she apologized, maybe Payne would let her interview his employees. That was a 'Hail Mary' pass for sure. She envisioned herself groveling to Payne and crinkled her nose before shuddering. Her phone rang.

"This is Cruz. Yes, sir..." she glimpsed Ashford, "yes, he's right here. We're on our way, sir." She dropped the handset onto the base and stood. "Jameson wants to see us."

. . .

Maintaining a regular exercise regimen of lifting weights and jogging, the fifty-year-old Director of the Federal Bureau of Investigation, Phillip Jameson, was physically fit. He stood five-feet, eleven inches tall and weighed one hundred and ninety pounds. The thick black frames of his rounded, rectangular eyeglasses stuck out against his baldhead. Dressed in a black suit, white shirt and red tie, his demeanor was all business.

Having spent many years with the FBI in various capacities, he was well known and respected among his peers. His climb to the top of the agency ladder had been a quick process. When James Conklin became the President of the United States, he had a list of potential candidates to head the FBI. One name was on it—Phillip Jameson. The two became friends and the President gave Jameson a wide berth in leading the nation's premier investigation agency. For his part, Jameson did not squander his opportunity, or the President's confidence. He demanded the same integrity from his agents that he had shown throughout his career. Whether or not his agents liked him, all of them revered the man.

Jameson heard the expected rap on his open door. He lifted his head and motioned for his visitors to enter. "Come in and shut the door."

Cruz and Ashford took their seats in front of Jameson's desk. Her partner was to her left. Both of them waited for their boss, who was typing on his computer's keyboard. Lifting his hand a little higher, Jameson punctuated his last keystroke before squaring his shoulders with his agents. "Can either of you tell me why I received a phone call from Senator Payne—Walter Payne—from Virginia?"

Cruz turned toward Ashford, who made a face and shrugged. "I don't think we can, sir."

Jameson clasped his hands and rested them on the desk. "The Senator is demanding that I reprimand the two of you and cease all contact with his brother, Henry Payne, on the grounds that you've been harassing the man, bursting into his office and verbally attacking him. Is this true?"

Cruz closed her eyes and tilted her head backward. Fixing her gaze on Jameson, she swallowed. "Sir, we had a nine o'clock meeting with him this morning. He kept us waiting for more than half an hour and—"

"You burst into his office."

She nodded. "But, neither of us attacked him, verbally or otherwise. We were questioning him about the Wilson murder case and he was impeding our investigation."

"How," Jameson shot back?

"For starters, he refused to tell us what Jason and Jane Wilson were working on when they were killed."

"Did you have a warrant?"

Cruz shook her head and said, "No, sir."

"Then, he doesn't have to tell you anything." Jameson rotated his hands outward and raised his eyebrows. "What's going on here? This isn't like you two. I know you went through a lot last night, Agent Cruz, but you assured me you were capable of fulfilling your duties. Is that still the case?" He held her gaze before adding, "Do you need some time off?"

She flexed her jaw muscles. Her lips disappeared into her mouth. *No, I don't need any time off. What I need is to find the sons-of-*...she drew a deep breath, let it out and steamrolled over the personal question, redirecting the conversation toward Payne. "I don't have any evidence, but my gut tells me Henry Payne is somehow involved in the Wilson murders. At the very least, he knows more than he's telling. I realize a gut feeling means nothing in the eyes of the law, but we can't get evidence if Payne keeps putting up roadblocks." She pointed toward Jameson's phone. "The fact that he got his brother involved says *something*. He's trying to keep us from doing our jobs." Cruz folded her hands in her lap and glanced downward. "I'm telling you, sir, he's dirty."

Jameson eyed his agent. He liked her. More importantly, he respected her judgment. On numerous occasions, she had proven her gut instincts were worth the benefit of his doubt. "What's your plan going forward?"

Cruz shifted in her chair. "I want to contact those who served with our killers...see if they can point us toward a common denominator, someone who may be coordinating the hits." She gestured. "Keep working our way up the ladder."

Jameson slowly nodded and shifted his eyes toward his phone. He came back to Cruz. "You've got twenty-four hours." He tilted his head toward the phone. "I can delay Senator Payne for that long. If you find something, but need more time, let me know. I have powerful connections, too. But...I'd rather not play that card if I don't have to."

Cruz realized he was referring to his relationship with the President. "I understand, sir. Thank you."

Jameson spun his chair and faced the computer. "Keep me informed of your progress, Agent Cruz."

She stood and nodded. "Yes sir."

Once they were out of the office and out of earshot, Ashford peeked over his shoulder. "I thought we were getting jerked from this case. Can you believe Payne, using his brother's pull like that?"

She jabbed her finger at the air between them. "He's crooked, Ash. I know it."

"Knowing it and *proving it* are two different things."

Striding toward her office, she spun her head to see him. "Then, let's go prove it."

7:32 P.M.

Dividing between them the list of ex-military members who had served with the killers, Special Agent Cruz and Ashford spent the afternoon tracking down the veterans. Showing the former service men a picture of the assassins, the agents questioned the men; most recognized their fellow soldiers, but none had had any recent contact with them.

"Yeah, I'm striking out, too, Ash." Cruz strode along the south side of Wilson Boulevard in Arlington, Virginia. A strong north wind was driving her sideways. She turned up the collar of her black overcoat and pressed her off hand to her ear, blocking the wind, so she could hear her partner. The three-inch heels of her black knee boots clopping against the concrete surface of the sidewalk, she jogged the last few feet to her destination, Arlington Rooftop Bar & Grill, before scurrying into the establishment. "I've got a few people left to check out on my list. I'll call you in an hour. Let me know if you get any hits." Unbuttoning her overcoat, she lifted the hem of her gray long-sleeved sweater and stuffed her mobile into the front pocket of her curve-hugging blue jeans. Knowing she was going to be spending a lot of time in the cold and snowy weather, she had stopped at her house and changed into appropriate clothing.

Spinning her head to the left and right, she spied the crowd. Most of the people were busy eating and chatting, while glancing at the numerous television screens along the wall. A few people sat alone, nursing a beverage and watching a sporting event. No one noticed her arrival. The atmosphere was loud. It was easy to get lost in the controlled chaos.

Cruz fanned the lapels of her overcoat, flinging snow onto the floor. Weaving in between tables and chairs, she made her way to the bar and found an empty chair, directly in front of a television showing a hockey game. Lifting her leg and butt cheek, she wiggled onto the dark wooden stool. Hooking the heels of her boots on the stool's rung, she situated herself and leaned forward, resting her forearms on the bar. After glancing up and down the length of the bar, she settled into watching the game. She had a basic understanding of the sport, but hockey was not her favorite thing to watch.

Since Cruz grew up in Dalhart, Texas, a small town named for its location near the border of Dallam and Hartley counties, she had been a lifelong fan of the Dallas Cowboys. Football was her chosen sport. At the age of ten, she saw her first game with her father. She still remembered the feeling. The deafening noise of the cheering fans, the perfect view—fifty-yard line and up enough rows to see over the players on the sideline—and the game itself had combined to hook her on the sport, and the team, forever. Yes, if the Cowboys did not make the playoffs, it was a long seven months until next year's preseason games started.

"What can I get you, miss?"

Cruz locked eyes with the bartender, a wide man with thick arms and a broad chest, standing six-feet tall and wearing a black polo shirt, the sleeves stretched taut above the bulging biceps. His dark hair was cropped in a military-style crew cut. If the haircut did not hint at his former profession, the square jaw, erect spine and piercing gaze filled out the resume. A glance at his nametag verified her suspicion. "I'll have a Coca Cola with light ice, please."

Thirty seconds later, the bartender returned and set the beverage on a square napkin. "Will that be all?"

"Carlos Ruiz?" Cruz questioned.

His left eye twitched. "Who's asking?"

She lifted her sweater, revealing the badge on her belt and a portion of the adjacent firearm. "Special Agent DelaCruz of the FBI," she said. Leaning forward and maintaining eye contact, she slid a piece of paper across the bar. The photos of the two assassins were on it. "Do you know these men?"

Ruiz dropped his eyes to the photos. He scrunched up his face and answered, "Nope," before sliding the paper back.

Cruz read the man's face. When people lied, their

words did not betray them. How they said the words and their facial clues gave them away. During her time with the FBI, she had perfected the art of detecting when someone was lying to her. This man had sent her three signals in less than a second. "Are you sure about that, Mr. Ruiz?" She pushed the paper back. "Please take another look."

Ruiz placed both hands on the bar and squinted at her. "I don't need to take another look. I told you I don't know them."

Having served in the military, she knew the code soldiers lived and died by—never leave a man behind. That code extended to not selling out one another, too. She tried to appeal to his code of ethics. "Look, I was in the military, too. I understand you want to protect your friends. I'd do the same thing if I were in your shoes. But, I really need to know if you've seen them recently and if anyone was with them."

He arched his back and compressed his eyebrows. "*You* were in the military?"

She nodded.

Ruiz shot out a puff of air between his pursed lips and said, "What branch?"

Cruz took a sip of soft drink and returned the glass to its spot on the bar. She swallowed. "The same as you," she said, lifting a finger toward him. "I never saw combat, though."

Ruiz grinned. "Of course not...you were a powder-

   DEFENSE OF INNOCENTS

puff secretary."

Sensing a sliver of camaraderie forming between them, she chuckled. "Yeah the whole no-women-in-combat stick Uncle Sam has up his butt kept me from seeing action. I'm allowed to die as an FBI agent, but not as a soldier."

"How long ago did you serve?"

"It's been almost ten years." She pointed at the photos with her chin. "What can you tell me about them?" She watched Ruiz gawk at her for close to a minute, trying to determine if she was telling the truth and deciding his next move. She had him on the fence. It was time to give him a nudge. "Mr. Ruiz, these men have murdered people. They broke into my home and tried to do the same to *me*."

His eyebrows went higher and he rotated his head a few degrees. "Tried?" he repeated.

"Yes, they're dead." She gestured toward the one on the left side of the paper. "I killed *him* and my neighbor helped with the other." She lifted her glass. "Am I still a powder puff?"

Ruiz crossed his arms over his chest. "I'm supposed to believe that *you* killed *Patton*?"

She twisted her free hand outward, "Do you need to see his body?" and took a drink.

The bartender regarded her for several moments before snatching the paper, leaning forward and resting his forearms on the bar. Glancing at the photos, he shook his head. "We called him," he motioned toward the image, "Patton...we called him Digger. It was short for Grave Digger. He put more insurgents in the ground than any two or three of us combined. He was one tough and mean S.O.B." He tilted his head to meet Cruz's gaze. "You said he murdered some people."

She nodded. "If I hadn't stopped him, he would've done the same to me and the little seven-year-old girl who was with me. Her parents were the ones he gunned down in cold blood." She let her words sink in for a few seconds. "She's seven and she's an orphan now, Mr. Ruiz. That's enough to make a decent person sick, don't you think?"

"I get it, Agent..."

"DelaCruz," she said, finishing his nonverbal inquiry.

"I get it, Agent DelaCruz. You can stop laying it on thick. And, call me Carlos." Ruiz straightened. "They were in here a couple days ago...Friday night I think. They had a couple of beers at the bar before a man showed up. The three of them took a seat over there," he pointed, "and stayed," Ruiz shrugged, "maybe half an hour. I'm not sure. I didn't see them leave. I just remember glancing over there and they were gone."

Cruz produced a notepad and pen. "You said they met a man. Did you get a name?"

Ruiz glanced away. "I think one of them called him...Michael or...Mick maybe."

Cruz scribbled. "What did he look like?"

After Cruz had written down the man's description and asked several additional questions, she stood and handed Ruiz a business card. "Thank you, Carlos. You've been a big help. If you think of anything else," she pointed toward the card, "please contact me." She retrieved a ten-dollar bill and put it on the counter. "Keep the rest."

"If you don't mind me asking," Ruiz tilted his head to the side, "How'd you kill Digger?"

Cruz did not relish taking another's life. It sometimes came with the job, but she never boasted about it. In fact, after saying a quick prayer for the deceased, she put the act out of her mind, turning everything, including her soul, over to God. She reconciled that as long as she lived she would never know why some people lived long and happy lives, while others perished at a young age. She trusted God and did not question his wisdom. She also knew that Ruiz wanted to know what happened to his brother-in-arms. She answered him flatly, "CQB...hand-to-hand."

Ruiz understood the acronym for close quarter battle and respected the way she had used the term. "I'm sorry, ma'am..." he extended his hand, "for the powder-puff comment. Anyone who can take down a man as skilled and dangerous as Digger deserves more respect than I showed you."

"Thank you, Carlos." She shook hands and left the

bar.

. . .

"The bartender remembers seeing our guys with someone Friday night. He gave me a rough description, but he's agreed to work with a sketch artist. The problem is his shift goes for another four hours. Can you get someone out here tonight to speed up the process?" Cruz had turned left and was heading down Barton Street. The wind was to her back, making it easier to hear her partner.

"That'll be my next call after I hang up." Ashford switched topics. "Hey, how are you holding up? You've been on the go all day with only a couple hours of sleep."

Cruz did not realize how tired she was, until he brought up the subject. In the past, she had worked cases with very little sleep, but this time was different. She could not put her finger on the cause. Perhaps the stress from repelling a brutal attack last night had taken an extra toll on her body. Whatever the reason, she was determined not to let sleeplessness get in the way of finding her prey. An image of Madison popped into her mind, and Cruz wondered how she was doing. The girl had witnessed the death of her parents—her father at least—yanked from her home and placed into protective custody. Thankfully, she had her grandparents to provide a little normalcy. Without realizing it, Cruz voiced her mental conversation. "I won't rest, until we've got every last one of them...and Madison and her grandparents can stop looking over their shoulder and start on building a better life."

"I agree with you there, Cruz, but you need to take care of yourself. You're no good to anyone if you can't function. Give me the last names on your list. I'll pay them a visit and you can head home for some shut-eye."

Cruz cleared the brick building on her left and hurried toward her car, located on the other side of a small parking lot. Grinning, she pushed aside a lock of hair that had separated from her midrise ponytail. On several occasions, Ashford had remarked that she treated him like her younger brother. The joking tone in his voice told her he was not upset. In fact, he seemed to take the 'protection' in stride. She chuckled at the role reversal. "I promise I'll be home by ten, Dad. Seriously, I'll call you when I'm on my way back."

Jamming the cell phone into the pocket her jeans, she pressed the key fob and the Charger's horn beeped once before the headlights flashed and the interior was lit. Rounding the left rear corner of the vehicle, she felt every aching muscle in her body. She stretched out her hand for the door handle. *Man, I'm beat. Maybe Ash was right. I need to get some shut—*" the hairs on the back of Cruz's neck shot up and a chilling sensation raced down her back. A split-second before she whipped her head to the left, she caught sight of a man's silhouette reflected in the vehicle's window.

Her mental synapses firing, Special Agent Cruz saw the thin wire zip by her eyes. The sudden movement of her head threw off her assailant's aim, allowing her to get a hand under the garrote wire. The device closed around her neck and the sleeve of her overcoat. The garment's leather protected her forearm. With her back to the man's belly and her neck and right arm trapped inside the taut metal loop, she took a giant step to the right, dipped her left shoulder and pivoted to the left, bringing her body perpendicular to the attacker. The razor wire dug into the left side of her neck. She shifted her eyes left and searched for a target.

The man howled in agony, released his grip and staggered backward, holding his hand to his face. Getting her left arm outside of his shoulders, Cruz had jammed her thumb into his right eye. She flung the free end of the killing tool away from her body and went on the offensive. The man's stance provided the first target. Her leg shot up, the shaft of her boot, an inch above the ankle, connecting with his groin. He grabbed the injured area and dropped to one knee. She lifted her right leg and thrust it toward his chest. He leaned to his right and avoided the strike before clutching her thigh in his armpit and springing to his feet. He charged, wrapped his right arm around her body and drove her backwards.

Cruz skipped on the heel of her left boot, until her back slammed into the side of the Charger. Her head recoiled and bounced off the roof. Everything went black. Tiny specks of light appeared and disappeared in an instant. With both arms free of his grasp, she simultaneously smacked his ears. He bellowed and his grip slackened. She chopped at both sides of his neck, where the torso connects. The arm curled around her leg went limp and she shoved him away. With a modicum of separation between them, she delivered an open hand strike, the palm of her right hand landing squarely under his chin. His head rocked backward and he staggered. She thrust the heel of her boot at the top of his left knee, hyperextending it. More screams escaped his mouth and he fell to one knee. Cruz balled her fist and nailed him with a hard left cross to his chin. His shoulders sagged and he keeled over, landing on wet and slushy snow.

Drawing her weapon, Cruz circled behind him. Using her boot, she pushed on his right shoulder blade and rolled him, until he was face-down in the slush. She hooked the left elbow with the toe of the same boot and jerked the arm out from under his body. Pulling handcuffs from the case on her belt, she lowered herself, her knee connecting with the back of the man's neck. She holstered her weapon, cuffed him and read him his rights. The ensuing string of vulgarities from his mouth told her his senses had returned.

Cruz got to her feet, leaned over and curled her

fingers around the chain between the handcuffs. "Insulting my mother and genitalia are not—" she clamped her teeth together, blinked her eyes several times and shook her head. She took a step backward, lost her balance and took a knee. She was spinning around in circles. No, the world around her was spinning. Either way, she was in trouble. Her peripheral vision was the first thing to go. The scene in front of her closed to a small circle. That same scene rotated to the right before her left shoulder slammed into the hard surface of the parking lot. Her vision went to black, while the sounds around her faded.

. . .

Opening her eyes, Cruz lifted her head and saw the small figure of a man, his feet to the left and his head to the right, in her line of sight. He sloughed along, getting smaller. She did not know how long she had been unconscious, but she recalled everything that had happened. She fumbled for her pistol. Closing her fingers around the butt, she freed the weapon from its holster and lined-up the gun's sights with the target—the middle of three identical images of a man moving away. Her words barely audible to her own ears, she said, "Stop. Stay where you are." Not hearing her command or not caring, the fleeing man kept going. Her vision blurry, she could not take the shot. If she missed, she might hit an innocent civilian. Worse yet, she could hit the target and the target could be a civilian. She would have to let him get away.

A moment later, her vision sharpened and she saw the handcuffs on the limping man. He glanced over his shoulder before turning back around and picking up his pace. This might be her only opportunity. Closing her left eye and touching the trigger, she smoothly pulled her finger backward. After the fireball on the other side of the muzzle dispersed, she witnessed the man collapse onto the pavement. Seconds later, Cruz's world went dark. Still clutching the pistol, her hands fell, followed by her head.

. . .

Cruz's eyelids fluttered. Hearing far off voices, she felt a hand on her arm, gently shaking her body.

Man's voice—"Miss, are...okay? Miss, can...hear me?"

Woman's voice—"Be careful...She has...gun."

Man's voice—"Look...the badge...a cop."

Second man's voice—"Hey, check out...He's handcuffed...She must've arrested..."

. . .

Cruz saw herself and Madison playing on a swing set. A high heel shoe flew across a field of stones. The little girl squealed and the vision was gone. Cruz sensed her body rolling back and forth.

Man's voice—"Her vital signs are...except for...pressure—it's low. She has a gash...her neck. Inform...she's lost blood, but I can't...We're on our way...Light it up...let's move."

Hearing a siren wailing, Cruz opened her eyes. A second later, a man's face entered her line of sight.

"Hello, Raychel. I'm Robert...an EMT...We're taking you..."

. . .

Cruz saw her kitchen. She and Madison were tossing flour at each other. They were covered in white powder, laughing. She felt a prick on her neck and the dream ended.

Man's voice—"Pull back the gauze and..."

She half-opened her eyes and glimpsed a flurry of activity. Bright lights were overhead. Varying in tone, loudness and duration, beeping noises sounded in both ears.

Woman's voice—"Yes, doctor."

Cruz got a fuzzy image of a woman wearing a white mask over her nose and mouth.

Woman's voice—"It's okay, dear. You're...fine...just need to stitch...wound...giving you a local anesthetic..."

Cruz's eyelids fell. *Thanks...for the warn...*

March 22ND, 9:51 A.M.
Virginia Hospital Center
Arlington, Virginia

Special Agent Cruz slowly opened her eyes. A dim light was coming from behind her head. To her left, a rhythmic beeping noise was coupled with a growing pressure on her arm. Far away, a muffled voice over a loud speaker announced activity happening in room 201. The pressure on her arm released, followed by the sound of air being expelled.

Her last dream showed her saying goodbye to Madison at the safe house. The sadness she had felt at the time accompanied the image. Cruz rolled her eyes to the right.

Curtis Ashford sat in a chair, thumbing through a magazine, his legs crossed and his body slouching. He pivoted his head toward the door when he heard a voice over a loud speaker: *Doctor Sampson to room 201—STAT. Doctor Sampson to room 201—STAT.* Ashford did not know much about hospital jargon, but he knew the term STAT was not good. He heard the person in the bed clear her throat.

Cruz's voice was raspy and her sentences came out slowly. "You never cease to amaze me, Ash." She coughed.

"I didn't know...you liked Woman's Life." She watched him toss the magazine aside and stand. "I'll be sure to get you a..." more coughing, "subscription for Christmas."

Ashford joined her at the side of the bed, smiling. He tilted his head toward the discarded magazine. "It's the only thing they had available." Jutting out his chin, he added, "How are you feeling?"

Cruz took a moment to assess her condition in light of his question. She touched the back of her head. "My head hurts and my body feels banged up, but," she nodded her head and glanced up at him, "I feel pretty good." Her words were stronger and steadier. "I guess all I needed was a couple hours of sleep." She rubbed her eyes, while shuffling her feet under the blanket to relieve pressure points. Hearing her partner laugh, she pulled her hands away from her face and turned toward him. "What's so funny?"

He spied his watch. "Cruz, it's almost ten o'clock in the morning...*Tuesday* morning. You've been out for nearly twelve hours."

Her eyes bulged. "What? I've got to get out of here." She pushed her upper body away from the mattress, threw back the covers and slid a bare leg over the bedrail.

Ashford placed a hand on her chest and eased her back into a prone position before cupping her calf and returning the leg to its previous spot. "Absolutely not," he asserted. "You're not going anywhere, until the doctor gives you a clean bill of health." Drawing the covers back over her body, he sensed her glare. "You can get angry all you want, Cruz. This is one time you're going to listen to me."

She squinted and her lips formed a straight line. "I'm the lead agent. I could just give you a direct order, you know."

Ashford pursed his lips and shook his head. "You *could*, but it wouldn't matter."

"Oh," she responded, arching her eyebrows. "Why's that?"

He stood erect and said, "Because I'm bigger and stronger than you."

"So were the two men who attacked me." She brought her eyebrows together and touched her forefinger to the corner of her lips. "How exactly did that work out for them again?"

Ashford could not suppress the grin. She had been awake only for a minute and her wit and humor was razor sharp.

"Since I'm *apparently* not going anywhere, care to tell me what happened?" She took in the room's décor. "How'd I get here? What about the man I arrested? Did he get away?"

"What do you remember?"

Cruz's head hit the pillow. She stared at the ceiling. After a moment, she recanted her story, beginning at the point where she ended the call with Ashford. "And, I woke up to find you," she shot a finger toward the chair behind him, "sitting over there."

"Well, I spoke with the officers at the scene and they told me some civilians found you unconscious in the parking lot near your car...which I had a couple agents drive to your home." He took a breath.

"Thank you."

"The civvies called 9-1-1, while others held down the man you arrested."

"Do we have an ID yet? What about—"

Ashford held up his hand. She had a penchant for asking multiple questions at once. "He—Mitchell Dawson—was handcuffed and bleeding from a gunshot wound to the leg. He tried to escape, but couldn't get very far with his hands behind his back and the bum leg."

"What do we know about him?"

Ashford ignored the question. "EMT's brought you in and the doctor took care of your wound. They've been monitoring you throughout the night. The doctor says you were lucky." He poked the left side of his neck. "If that wire had gone deeper, you'd have—" he caught himself before his voice had a chance to break, "bled out in seconds."

Cruz heard the crack. "You've been here all night with me, haven't you?"

Ashford folded his arms across his chest. "Cruz, you were suffering from exhaustion. Outside of the two hours of sleep you got early Monday morning, you were awake for almost thirty-six hours straight. In that time, you were involved in *two* hand-to-hand battles for survival." He jerked his thumb toward the door. "Based on what the doctor has told me, your body decided it had had enough," his hands moved outward like an umpire calling a base runner safe, "and just shut down. If you hadn't slapped the cuffs on Dawson," Ashford took her hand, "he'd have killed you." He paused. "You were lucky indeed."

Cruz regarded her partner. He had never shown this much emotion in the time they had worked together. He portrayed the persona of macho man, but she knew he had a softer, sentimental side few people were allowed to see. She squeezed his hand and flashed a smile. "God was definitely looking out for me. That's for sure."

The door opened and a man in a white lab coat entered the room. "Good morning, Miss DelaCruz. How are you feeling?" He approached the bed, holding a clipboard.

"I'm feeling much better, Doctor..." she flicked her eyes toward his badge, "Austin. When can I get out of here?"

He chuckled. His head pivoted, while he wrote the numbers from a machine on his clipboard. "I figured you might ask me that." He clicked the pen and stuck it into his shirt pocket. "I want to keep an eye on your vital signs for a bit longer. They're all good, but I just want to monitor them for a few more hours." He scrunched his face and bobbed his head. "I think you should be discharged by early afternoon at the latest." He smiled.

Cruz frowned and opened her mouth to protest.

Ashford leaned in and cut her off, touching her shoulder with one hand and her forearm with the other. "Thank you, doctor, that'll be just fine. She's been looking forward to catching up on her sleep."

Doctor Austin noted the exchange and half grinned before turning to leave.

"I'm hungry, doctor. Is there any chance I can get something to eat?"

"Of course," he replied, returning and handing her a menu. "You can call the number on the front and place your order. It might be quicker, however, if your friend goes to the cafeteria downstairs and gets you something." He shifted his gaze to Ashford. "Stick to mild and bland foods. We don't want to upset her system." After a short laugh, he added, "Since this is a hospital, it shouldn't be too difficult to find food that meets those criteria."

Cruz laughed before wincing when a lightning bolt of pain snaked its way up her back. She liked the man. "Thank you, doctor."

On his way to the door, Doctor Austin raised his hand. "If you don't see me again, that'll be a good thing. Take care of yourself, Miss DelaCruz."

The door closed and Ashford focused on Cruz. "So, what can I get you for lunch? It's my treat."

She shot out a puff of air and curled up the right side of her mouth. "Where's that generosity when we stop for lunch at a nice restaurant?" She pushed her body further up the mattress. "Before you go, tell me about Mitchell Dawson."

1:48 P.M.
J. EDGAR HOOVER BUILDING
WASHINGTON, D.C.

Looking through the one-way glass into the interrogation room, Special Agent Cruz, Ashford and Director Jameson watched and listened to the agent questioning Mitchell Dawson. Dawson sat in a metal chair, his wrists handcuffed and shackled to an eyebolt attached to a table, which was bolted to the floor. The agent asked question after question. Dawson said nothing.

Ashford put his hands on his hips. "This is useless." Not taking his eyes off Dawson, he rotated his head to his right and spoke to Cruz. "He's been in there for hours and he hasn't said two words. I say we take a two-by-four in there and ask the same questions. Just give me ten minutes and I guarantee he'll be more forthcoming with information."

On the other side of Cruz, Jameson's stoic face showed his displeasure with Ashford's words. "That's not how we do things here, Agent Ashford. I expect the utmost professionalism from you at all times." His eyes dropped. "You've been quiet, Agent Cruz...any thoughts?"

She stood with her arms folded, weight shifted to her

right foot, her gaze penetrating through the pane. "Do we have any leverage on him? Anything at all that even comes close to showing ties to his employer?"

Ashford shook his head. "We haven't found anything. He has a couple of financial accounts, but there's only about ten thousand dollars in them, combined. The cost for a hit of this magnitude would be a lot higher than that. There's no digital trail. I'm sure he used cash to pay his men and his employer did the same to pay him."

"What about residences or property?"

"He has an apartment in Virginia and a couple storage units a few miles away. Agents have scoured everything, but turned up nothing. Even if they *did* find a large sum of money, it's cash. Cash can't be traced back to the person who gave it to him." Ashford's forefinger touched the glass. "He knows we can't link him to the Wilson murders or to the person who hired him. He also knows if he keeps his mouth shut, we won't be able to add to the charges already leveled against him. He's a real pro."

Cruz stared at the man responsible for two failed assassination attempts on her life, one indirectly and one directly. His failure had to be gnawing at him. As Ashford had put it, Dawson was a pro and professionals *hated* failing. After a few moments of silence, she spoke to the glass. "I want a shot at him, sir."

Cupping his right elbow in his hand, Jameson stroked his chin before sending a sideways glance her way. "Are you sure about that? What makes you think he'll talk to you?"

"I have something the other agents don't have." She tapped her chest with her fingertips. "I'm the reason he's in there."

. . .

Closing the door to the interrogation room, Cruz made a slow and methodical lap around Dawson, each footfall from her knee boots echoing off the concrete walls. Stopping in front of him, she leaned forward and grabbed the back of the empty chair on the opposite side of the table from Dawson. Glimpsing the thick white bandage over his right eye, she gestured with her chin. "How's the eye?" No response came. "What about your leg? You have to admit that was a really good shot, all things considered." His face was deadpan, but Cruz caught a facial tick. He was getting angry. Anger was good. The emotion of anger tended to overrule logical thought processes.

She spun the chair, spread her legs and sat, resting her crossed forearms on the chair's back. Using her thumb, she scratched the bottom of her chin before holding up two fingers. "You sent two thugs to kill me." She paused. "*They* failed." She pointed. "You cowardly snuck up from behind and tried to strangle me." More silence. "*You* failed." Cruz saw his left eye twitch. She shook her head. "You call yourself a professional, but with a resume like that..."

Cruz gaped at Dawson for more than a minute, the stillness creating an awkward pall in the air between them. The color of his cheeks went from flesh tone to crimson to bright red. His narrow eyes never strayed from her piercing gaze. She needed to loosen his tongue. Once that happened, answers would follow. She calculated embarrassment was the doorway through which she would get those answers. "How many people have you murdered, Mitch? Can I call you Mitch?" She nodded. "I feel we know each other well enough that I can call you Mitch. So, how many? I can imagine the number is quite high." She infused her words with sarcasm, reckoning it would rattle him. "You weren't up to the task of killing me—a *female*—were you, Mitch?" She sneered and held up her forefinger. "You had the element of surprise," the middle finger shot up, "a position of advantage," the ring finger joined the first two fingers, "and you outweighed me by what," she flicked her eyes up and down his frame, "at least fifty, seventy-five pounds." He drew his chin in and the muscles at the back of his jaw protruded. Cruz spotted his clenched fists. The knuckles were white. "Then, there's the matter of the defenseless little girl. Two big men couldn't do the job *you* hired them to do." She glanced around the room. "It's no wonder you're in here. A boss is only as good as the people he—"

Dawson leapt from his chair, the chains of his restraints stretched to the max. His open hands demonstrated how he would have enjoyed ending her life.

Cruz never flinched. She had anticipated, even hoped for, the move. His anger had superseded his reason.

Straining against the shackles, his face burning with rage, Dawson growled, "Give me one more chance and I'll show you what I'm capable of doing to that pretty little neck of yours."

She smirked and maintained an even tone of voice. "I'm afraid that's not going to happen, Mitch. You've had your chance—*two chances* in fact." She leaned closer, an inch from his outstretched fingertips. "And...you...screwed...up. Now, you're going to go away for a long, long time. Attempted murder of a federal agent carries a hefty price tag."

Dawson transformed his hands into fists. The muscles in his forearms quivered, while he lowered his body into the chair. "I had you. If you hadn't turned your head at the last second, I would've sliced your neck open and watched you choke on your own blood."

Cruz shrugged. "Would've, should've...the bottom line is," she pointed toward herself, "I'm over here," she gestured toward Dawson, "and you're over there, wearing steel bracelets. Face it, Mitch. You lost and I won. And, you'll have to live with that, while you're rotting in a stinking cell in a federal prison somewhere." A few moments passed. "However, the stench and the prison don't have to be that bad."

Cruz straightened in the chair, her spine erect. "The

way I see it," she held up one finger, "you've got one card to play here." His v-shaped eyebrows told her she had his attention. "Tell us who hired you for the Wilson murders, and I'll do what I can to get you sent somewhere *not as bad*. My offer only lasts for as long as I'm in this room."

Dawson scoffed.

"If you think I'm bluffing, try me." She extended her left arm. "After that door closes and I'm gone, I'll do everything in my power to make sure you call home the *worst* our federal penitentiary system has to offer." Cruz watched his eyes drop and study the table. "Even without your help, I'm going to find the person or persons responsible for those murders...and the attempt on *my* life. You've tussled with me, Mitch. You know I don't give up easily. Do yourself a favor. Make a deal. Give me a name."

Several minutes of silence passed. Cruz thought she had him on the ropes, ready to crack and bargain for a better arrangement; however, his hardened face told her she had miscalculated. Standing, she headed for the door. "All right, if that's the way you want to play it..." When she reached for the doorknob, she half expected him to call out to her. Inwardly, she chuckled. *That's what always happens in the movies.* Dawson was calling her bluff, however, and the gamble was going to cost him. She had picked out the perfect prison for him. Throwing open the door, she stepped into the hallway, her mind evaluating all options to find whoever hired Dawson. The door was less than a foot from shutting when the man's booming voice beckoned her.

4:27 P.M.

The elevator door opened. Special Agent Cruz and Ashford emerged and spun left, followed by four additional agents, who were wearing full tactical gear and carrying 5.56 mm rifles. Hearing the commotion, Greta Patrick whipped her head toward the elevator. Her shoulder-length red hair flew over her right shoulder, making Ashford's wish come true—seeing her with her hair down. Patrick stood.

Making a beeline for Henry Payne's office door, Cruz locked eyes with the secretary. "Don't even think about it." Addressing the tactical unit, she added, "Gentlemen, if she takes a single step forward, arrest her for obstruction of justice. No one enters this room, unless I say so." She barged through the door, Ashford and three members of the unit on her heels.

The last member of the unit spun around and put his back to the doorway. "Yes, ma'am," he responded.

Payne was talking on the phone. Startled by the intrusion, he jumped to his feet and reached for something on his desk. The move almost cost him his life.

Cruz and Ashford presented their weapons and shouted, "Freeze—don't move." Cruz motioned left and right and the heavily armed men spread out, taking up positions of fire on either side of the desk.

"What's the meaning of this?" Payne's voice broke, but he squared his shoulders with Cruz. "Agent DelaCruz, you have—"

"Hands," she yelled, creeping closer to the desk. "I need to see those hands, Mr. Payne...*now*."

Payne pivoted his head right and left, a scowl on his face.

"Drop the phone and raise your hands," Cruz commanded.

Surrounded by five people, the muzzles of their weapons directed at him, Payne complied.

Seconds later, the first handcuff clamped onto his wrist. "Why am I being arrested? What are the charges, Agent DelaCruz?"

"The list is long, but the ones that stand out are the murder of Jason and Jane Wilson and the attempted murder of their daughter. Next on the list is conspiring to have a federal officer—*me*—killed."

"That's preposterous," countered Payne, his facing contorting when an overzealous agent closed the second steel cuff around his wrist. "I had nothing to do with any of that."

"I have a witness who says otherwise." Mitchell Dawson had given up Payne's name as the one who had hired him to do the jobs.

"Who is this witness? I have a right to know who my

accuser is." The agent who had cuffed Payne took hold of the man's elbow and guided him around the desk. "Talk to me, Agent DelaCruz. Who said I was involved?" The agent and Payne had cleared the corner of the desk and the two of them were crossing the Persian rug. Payne cranked his head over his shoulder. "Who was it?"

Cruz raised her hand. "Hold up."

The agent and Payne stopped. The CEO turned to face her.

She stood in front of him and read his face. He seemed genuinely confused, although the terror from being accused of murder could have been eliciting the emotion. "Mitchell Dawson said you hired him to kill the Wilsons. When the job was botched and he learned their daughter was still alive and could identify the killers, he sent them to my house to finish their work."

Payne lowered his shaking head. "No, no, no, I have no idea who this man is. I've never heard of a Mitchell...Dawson. I don't hire killers, Agent DelaCruz. Yes, this industry is cutthroat, but I would never stoop to such a thing. I and the rest of my staff..." he stopped ranting and stared at a distant corner of the office.

Cruz watched him.

His eyes darted back and forth, while his face turned white. "How did this Mitchell Dawson say he was paid?"

Cruz did not have to answer the question. Her job was to make the arrest. Lawyers would take the case from there. Her keen ability to read people, however, was overriding her other senses. Her gut instinct was telling her there was something more to this man's behavior. He was not acting like a criminal who had been caught. She indulged his curiosity. "He said you went through your assistant, Charles Patterson. He's also wanted. Where can we find him?"

Payne shut his eyes, expelled a huge breath of air and let his head hang down to his chest. "I haven't been able to contact him since yesterday morning. He left right before lunch. He said he had a luncheon meeting somewhere. Every call I placed to him went nowhere. It was like he didn't have a cell phone at all." Payne shook his head and spoke softly, sounding like a man who had received news from his doctor, telling him he had only months to live. "I can't believe it. I just can't believe it."

"What is it, Mr. Payne? What aren't you telling me? If you know where Mr. Patterson is, you could help your case. Withholding information will only make things worse for you."

Payne stared at Cruz. "I don't know where he is, but I can tell you everything I know." He brought his cuffed hands out from behind his back, tilted his head toward them and held her gaze.

Cruz let several moments pass before she nodded her head at the agent holding Payne's arm.

8:58 P.M.
DULLES INTERNATIONAL AIRPORT
DULLES, VIRGINIA

"This is the captain speaking. We have been cleared for takeoff. Please fasten your seatbelts and turn off all electronic devices. Thank you and have a nice flight."

Charles Patterson clamped together the ends of his seatbelt and got comfortable, which was easier to do in first class seating. He leaned right from his aisle seat to get a better view of the flight attendant's tanned legs. She was a gorgeous blonde specimen, who had been giving him special attention since he had taken his seat. He checked his watch. Less than twenty-four hours had passed since he had spent a couple of hours with a server from Jaleo.

After Dawson had left the restaurant, Patterson had asked her out, the two of them ending up at her place later that night. *What was her name...Esther...Emily?* He grinned at the prospect of having a 'home and home' with a woman with jet-black hair followed by a blonde-haired woman. Patterson had adapted the expression to fit his lifestyle. A 'home and home' was a hockey term that meant two games played between the same teams on two successive nights, one at each team's arena.

He returned to an upright position and closed his eyes before letting his head fall against the headrest. This was the final leg of his journey. In a few hours, he would have more money than he could spend in a lifetime, although he was certainly going to try. He mused at how easy it had been to deceive everyone. His military training had taught him how to play to people's weaknesses, getting them to think he was something other than what he truly was. The Ivy League accent rarely failed him. Whenever people heard it, they automatically assumed he was a rich snob with no street smarts. Most times, those people realized their mistake only moments before their demise.

Patterson's mind went back to his meeting with Dawson, specifically, his performance of a scared little man, outclassed and outmatched by a ruthless killer. Patterson let out a chuckle. Had it been necessary, he could have killed Dawson at his leisure, snuck up on him when he went to the men's room at Jaleo. Patterson had been in the restaurant when Dawson took his seat at the booth. After watching the man for half an hour, Patterson left and made his approach to the restaurant from across the street. Stopping traffic as he crossed had guaranteed his contact would see him coming, providing the man with a false sense of security and dominance. Charles Patterson had been in control of the entire situation.

Patterson felt the taxiing aircraft slow before coming to a stop. The captain's voice was heard. "Ladies and gentlemen, this is the captain speaking. We are experiencing...technical difficulties. We have been informed to stay on the runway. I apologize for any inconvenience. I will update you when I know more. Thank you for your patience."

. . .

The past thirty minutes had been stressful for Patterson. A stop on the runway was a common occurrence. Unexpected things happened all the time, causing aircraft to be delayed or head back to a terminal. His training, however, had taught him to be cautious, even when caution was not necessary. He saw the blonde flight attendant coming from the cockpit. He smiled. "Excuse me, Miss—"

She shot him down with barely a passing acknowledgement. "Everything's fine, sir. We should be taking off soon." She scurried down the aisle and slipped between the curtains separating first class seating from the rest of the passengers.

The hairs on the back of his neck stood up. *Sir? Half an hour ago, she was all over me, her body language practically begging me to join her in the bathroom.* He leaned over the adjacent seat and peered out the window. It was too dark to see anything. Sitting upright, he caught a glimpse of the left half of a woman's face near the cockpit door and his heart leapt into his throat. He had never met her, but he had seen her picture. *Damn it. How the hell did she find me?* Watching the woman casually slide her head back behind cover, he grabbed a spoon from the serving tray and clutched it in his hand. *Now it's going to get ugly.*

Grasping her Glock 23 with both hands, Special Agent Cruz charged into first class seating, shouting, "Go—Go—Go!" The heavily armed SWAT team stormed in from the opposite end. Startled passengers, whose minds were not engrossed in their electronic devices, ducked for cover, diving between the seats. Special Agent Cruz was grateful for their quick-thinking actions. The fewer people in the line of fire the better. "Everybody down," she yelled, as she brought her weapon to bear, training the front sight on whatever sliver of Patterson's body she could see. Hearing the command, the remaining upright travelers sought cover. "It's over, Patterson. You can't escape. Just let her go and everybody walks away alive."

Charles Patterson had done everything by the book, except for one thing. He paid for his plane ticket *before* he shut off his phone and removed the battery. A search of the cell phone towers showed his recent locations, including the travel agency where he bought the ticket, paying in cash. When shown his picture, a consultant at the agency confirmed the transaction, which led the FBI to this flight.

Cruz saw the SWAT members stacking behind the assailant. There was no room for them to spread out. She sensed Ashford's presence to her right. The remaining SWAT members were somewhere behind her. "Don't be stupid, Patterson. You have no endgame here."

Patterson held firm to the throat of the woman, the same woman he was fantasizing about less than an hour ago. His head appeared to be on a swivel, as he eyed his attackers. Keeping the woman close, he was confident he could buy time to figure out a strategy. He almost burst into laughter at the thought. There were not too many plans to deal with one against eight in the close confines of an aircraft. His mind worked overtime to come up with a solution. Whipping his head back toward the curtains, he noticed the lead SWAT member was inching closer. Inwardly, he smiled. He had his plan. Pivoting his head toward the front of the aircraft, he kept the approaching SWAT member in his peripheral vision. *I just need one more step.*

Cruz noticed Patterson's facial expression change. He was relaxed. No, he was preparing for something. She glanced beyond Patterson and saw Brooks had crept to within striking distance of Patterson. "Brooks, get back," she shouted. Before she had finished her warning, the target struck.

Patterson let go of the attendant and delivered a reverse roundhouse kick, connecting with the lead SWAT member's rifle, spinning the weapon and the man's body toward the port side of the airplane. A three-round burst filled the cabin, one bullet shattering a window. In one fluid motion, Patterson lunged forward, grabbed the man's sidearm and shot the federal officer in the head, below the helmet. A gut-twisting spray of blood, bone and brain matter splattered the ceiling, walls, windows and passengers. Using the dead man's body as a shield, he fired multiple rounds at the remaining men near the curtains.

Realizing she could not contain the coming firefight, Cruz clamped onto the flight attendant's shoulders and dove to the right. The interior of the plane erupted. The cacophony of multiple nine-millimeter MP5 rifles firing in the enclosed space had a disorienting effect. The fight lasted only a few seconds, but the ringing in her ears would last much longer. Cruz got to her feet and extended her pistol toward the spot where Patterson had been standing. He was on the floor, his body perforated by numerous bullets, leaving red holes in their wake.

She spun around, frantically searching for Ashford. Squatting in front of the first seat, he flashed the 'thumbs-up' sign. After affirming the safety of the two men with him, she sidestepped into the aisle, leapt over Patterson's body and hurried toward Brooks. She knew he was dead before she knelt beside his body. With the muzzle of her Glock 23 trained on Patterson, she felt for a pulse on Brooks. Lifting her head, she counted three standing SWAT members ahead of her. One was holding his limp arm at his side. The nearest member of the team flipped Patterson to his belly, cuffed him and looked up at her. She felt his eyes penetrating to the back of her skull. Slowly, she pivoted her head back and forth a fraction of an inch.

Standing, she holstered her weapon and observed the passengers, who were making their way to their feet and knees. "Is anyone injured?" She felt Ashford and another man brush by her to help the wounded. None appeared to be hurt, only shaken. Cruz lowered her head toward the body of Brooks and closed her eyes. She made the sign of the cross and said a prayer. She swept the fingers of both hands over her cheeks and wiped the moisture on her jeans. Slipping out of her overcoat, she went to one knee and covered the body of the fallen SWAT member.

MARCH 23RD, 8:38 P.M.
SEATTLE, WASHINGTON
SKY CITY RESTAURANT

Coulson brought the champagne glass to his lips. The precious liquid cascaded over his tongue, sending endorphins to his brain. He had never tasted money. If he had, however, he was sure the flavor of wealth would have matched the signals his taste buds were experiencing. A year ago, Coulson purchased a bottle of vintage Dom Pérignon at an auction house, paying nearly ten thousand dollars for two bottles. The gluttonous display of both power and money was a necessity for a man of his stature. Tonight he was celebrating. What better way to do so, he thought, than with the world's best champagne.

Ranking eleventh on the list of highest paid CEO's in the drug business, Edward J. Coulson, CEO of Coulson-Hayes Pharmaceuticals (CHP), made thirty-five million dollars last year. This year, his contract was up for renegotiation and he was maneuvering to strike a deal worth nearly double his current salary. Under his leadership, CHP had brought to market five new drugs, tripling the company's net worth and making its stockholders very rich. He had them right where he wanted them. How could they *not* succumb to his salary demands?

Coulson returned the glass to the table and peered out the windows of the restaurant, located inside Seattle's Space Needle, nearly six hundred feet off the ground. A breathtaking view of downtown Seattle lay beyond the clear windows. The sun had set over an hour ago and the tall buildings, varying in height, were awash with lights, creating a citywide year-round Christmas tree. Coulson marveled at the sight. This was the perfect place to celebrate his success. He had paid a small fortune to have the restaurant to himself for the evening. Yes, he was living large, enjoying every pleasure life afforded to the affluent inhabitants of the planet.

"Mr. Coulson, your guest has arrived. Shall I send him in?"

Coulson cranked his head away from the window and acknowledged the man who was his personal servant for the night. "Yes, Antonio, please," Coulson replied, reaching for his drink. He shut his eyes, brought the glass to his nose and breathed deeply. He smiled and opened his eyes. Spotting his guest strolling across the restaurant, his smile vanished and the champagne glass almost slipped between his fingers—a blunder that would have spilled several hundred dollars onto the white tablecloth.

Dressed in a black suit with a white shirt and a blue tie, Henry Payne slid into the booth across from Coulson. "Hello, old friend. I see you're doing well these days." He spun the champagne bottle. Ice cubes shifted in the bucket. Letting out a low whistle, he regarded Coulson and added, "*Very* well indeed."

Coulson stared at his former business partner, his jaw slightly agape.

"Mr. Patterson will not be joining you tonight, Edward." He situated himself on the seat. "I'm afraid he met his demise on an aircraft last night...at the hands of the Federal Bureau of Investigation."

An attractive woman approached the table. He glanced at her before his eyes dropped to her feet. She wore three-inch black stilettos, tan-colored nylons, a skimpy miniskirt and a white button-up collared shirt. The top three buttons were undone, revealing a hint of cleavage. Her long dark hair was tied loosely at the back of her head. Her pretty face sported oversized black eyeglasses that appeared to be more of a fashion statement than a medical necessity. He remembered Coulson had a penchant for placing an order for what his female servers would wear when they waited on him.

"Excuse me, Mr. Coulson, your dinner will be out shortly." She leaned over the ice bucket to grab an empty plate, lifting her leg off the floor. The stiletto stopped a few inches short of her skirt. She took a few extra seconds to gather a second plate and stack them on top of each other.

Payne watched Coulson ogle the woman's legs.

She straightened, put her hand on Coulson's shoulder

and met his gaze, tilting her head. Locks of hair had separated from the knot, flowing down either side of her face and neck. She flipped her head toward Payne before coming back to the one paying her wage for the evening. "Is there anything I can get either of you?"

Coulson's eyes shot down the length of her body and back up again. A grin, or a smirk, formed on his face. "Not right now, but maybe later, Sweetheart."

Feeling a hand along her leg, the woman giggled and dodged his advance. "I'll be right back, sir."

Payne poured a glass of the expensive fare and sampled it. "You still have excellent taste." He brought the glass to his nose. "This is *superb*." He placed the flute on the table and wiped his mouth with a heavy linen napkin. "What was I saying? Oh yes, Patterson...it's a shame what happened to him. He was my most trusted assistant." Payne locked eyes with Coulson and curled up the right side of his mouth. "But, you already knew that."

Coulson glared. "What the hell are you doing here? And, more importantly, how did you know I was going to be here?" He held up his hand before his counterpart could reply. He motioned and a man hurried to the table. "Sweep him," commanded Coulson.

"Sir, we checked him for bugs at the door," the man stammered.

"I don't give a damn." He motioned across the table. "Do it again. That's why I pay you...to do whatever I tell you to do. Now run that damn wand over him. I want to hear for myself."

Once the man had ran the electronic device over Payne's body, checking for listening gadgets, he waited for his boss's approval.

Coulson waved him away. "Not that I don't trust you—" he paused. "Actually, that's exactly what it is. I *don't* trust you. So, what's the purpose of this visit?"

"I think we both know why I'm here." He poked a finger at his one-time colleague. "You stole something from me, Edward. And, I want it back."

Ten years ago, when they were partners running a drug company, the men had a disagreement. The argument led to a parting of ways. Coulson started his own company, bringing to market a new drug within the first few months. Payne had insisted the drug was his and brought a lawsuit against his former partner. The case was thrown out of court, but Payne had held the grudge for the last decade. If it were not for Payne's drug, Coulson would not have gotten the early lead in their race to the top of the industry.

Coulson scoffed. "When are you going to let that go, Henry? That happened years ago and we both know I came up with that drug," he leaned closer, "on...my...own."

Payne smiled through clenched teeth, his hand nearly breaking the champagne glass in his grasp. "You arrogant piece of work, you know that's a lie." He waved his hand as if he was swatting at a fly. "That's not why I'm here," he bobbed his head, "although it falls under the same category—*stealing*. No, I'm here to talk about CynerGest."

Payne shifted in the booth and sat straight. "Does that name ring any bells?"

Coulson's face was stoic.

"It should. Patterson stole the research for CynerGest, wiped clean every hard drive and burned every paper trail of its existence before he fled to meet *you*," he pointed at the table, "*here.*"

Coulson sipped the champagne. "I don't know what you're talking about."

Payne's face reddened. "Come off it, Ed." His finger shot across the table, stopping an inch from knocking over Coulson's wine glass. "I know it was you who stole my research. You also had Patterson kill the Wilsons to make sure no one could reproduce the drug. The FBI knows it, too. They were able to make the connections."

His lips forming a snarl, Coulson leaned forward, his voice calm. "If that's true, my friend, then why are *you* sitting there and not the FBI?"

Payne laughed and pivoted his head to take in the view of the city. "You're good. I'll give you that." He appeared to ponder the question. "They haven't been able to make the last connection...the one that leads back to you." Facing the window, he shifted his gaze to the left. "As you already know, the trail stops with Patterson. Speaking of him, how long has he been working for you?"

Coulson was quiet, only smiling slightly.

"You must have been paying him well." He pinched the stem of his glass and took a sip. Letting the champagne stay in his mouth for a few moments, he regarded the other man, lifting his brows and waiting for an answer.

Coulson squinted and cocked his head. "So, if you already have all the answers, my question is even more pressing. Why have you paid me this visit? You're a busy man, Henry, and Seattle is a long way from Virginia. Why come all this way just to float your theory?"

Several moments of silence passed, while Payne spun his champagne glass and stared at the table. He drew a deep breath and exhaled through his nose. "I guess I needed to know what happened. I needed to look you in the eye and see the betrayal. After all these years, why screw me *again*?" He interlocked his fingers and rested them on the table. "We were friends, Ed." He opened his hands. "That must count for something." His words elicited no response. "Do you realize I was almost arrested for the murder of Jason and Jane Wilson?"

Coulson twitched a shoulder. "Did you do it?"

Payne rocked backward in the booth. "Don't give me that crap." He held his arms out to his sides. "Your men have already scanned me." He motioned with his forefingers in the space between them. "It's just you and me. You owe me an explanation. It's the least you can do."

Coulson laughed and tossed his napkin onto the table. He owed this man nothing. This man had taken advantage of him and sued him. As far as Coulson was concerned, he wished the FBI had arrested Payne and sentenced him to life in prison. Justice would have been served. He studied his one-time friend. He looked older than he remembered. He looked tired and worn out. An emotion that rarely worked its way to the surface of Coulson's persona overtook him—pity.

Coulson dropped his elbows on the table and clasped his hands together. "Perhaps you do deserve an explanation...*not* because I owe you anything." His eyes scanned Payne as if he was looking at a homeless man. "I feel sorry for you, Henry. You used to be so confident," he pumped his fist, "so full of life." He held out his hands, palms up, and gestured across the table. "Look at you. You've been reduced to a pathetic, groveling man, searching for answers." He wringed his hands and savored the moment. "Do you want me to say I did it? Will that make you feel better? Will you be able to leave this place with a shred of your manhood still intact?" He paused to let his words linger between them.

A minute passed and the awkward tension built. Coulson grinned and leaned closer. He opened his mouth. His words began as a whisper then built to a crescendo. "I did it—all of it...including the hit on the girl and the FBI agent." He held out his hands and puffed out his chest. "It was all me. Are you happy to have the truth?

Will you be able to go to sleep now?" He waved his hands at Payne as if he was shooing away a stray dog. "Get out of my sight, you feeble little man. I don't ever want to see your face again." He opened a napkin and placed it on his lap. "My dinner will be here soon and, frankly, the sight of you ruins my appetite."

As if on cue, the female server strode to the table with Coulson's meal. She set the plate in front of him and placed her hand on his shoulder, close to his neck. "Mr. Coulson, I'm here to make that happen for you."

He craned his head to see her. His eyebrows were drawn together. "Excuse me."

She motioned with her head toward Payne. "I guarantee you'll never have to see his face again." She held up her left hand and stuck an FBI badge in front of Coulson's nose. Her fingers plucked at the man's jacket collar before she held up a miniscule piece of equipment—the microphone had transmitted every word of the conversation to a recorder in the kitchen. "Edward J. Coulson, you're under arrest for the murders of Jason and Jane Wilson, the attempted murder of Madison Wilson and me, Special Agent DelaCruz." She handed the bug to Ashford, who had approached from behind her. Producing a pair of handcuffs, she grabbed Coulson's left arm and slammed the first cuff around his wrist. "You have the right to remain silent—"

"Wait a minute," Coulson boomed. "You have no proof I did any of those things." He held out his free hand toward Payne. "I was simply telling him what he wanted to hear. I never murdered anyone."

Cruz clamped her hand under his left arm. "Stand up, Mr. Coulson."

Ashford grabbed a fistful of the man's jacket from behind the booth. "No, please stay where you are and make this more difficult...please."

Cruz shot her partner a look. He was always ready for a fight. She took a step backward and pulled the suspect to his feet. She pushed him, until he was facing away from her. "Actually, we can, sir." Bringing the man's hands together, she locked the second cuff around his other wrist. With one hand on the chain between the cuffs and the other on Coulson's shoulder, she directed him toward Ashford. "Nobody knew about Madison, the little girl you tried to kill to cover up your deeds. And, nobody knew she was staying with me. That information was not shared with the media. The only way you could have known was if you were in contact with the killers or the man, Mitchell Dawson, who orchestrated the assassination attempts."

Coulson's head tipped backward. He had slipped and made a huge mistake.

"You were right," Cruz continued. "We had no way of pinning anything on you. You were good. You covered your tracks." She twirled a finger in the air over the table. "This little ruse was the only shot we had at getting you. I'm surprised you said *anything*." She handed control of the handcuffs to Ashford. "If you'd have just kept your mouth shut and had Mr. Payne escorted out of the restaurant, the FBI would have no case against you. In the end, I guess your arrogance and your contempt for Mr. Payne were your undoing, sir."

Coulson half turned his body. "How'd you even know to look in my direction?"

Payne interjected. "Please, Edward, it wasn't too difficult to connect the dots. Patterson's plane was landing in Seattle. Your headquarters are located in Seattle. I simply gave the FBI my best guess at who would want to steal secrets from me. You'd done it before. It wasn't much of a stretch." He nodded at Cruz. "The FBI did everything after that, including finding out when and where you were supposed to meet Patterson."

Coulson pivoted his body as far as he could, in order to view Payne. "So, in other words, you got *lucky*." He scoffed. "You never could do anything on your own. You always needed someone else's expertise."

Payne took a step toward Coulson.

Cruz put one hand on Payne's upper arm and the other on his shoulder. She broke his line of sight and shook her head. Keeping her eyes on Payne, she rotated her head and spoke to Ashford. "Get him out of here."

Ashford took charge of the suspect and hauled him away.

Cruz let go. "Mr. Payne, I owe you an apology."

He lowered his eyebrows and rocked his head

backward. "For what?" he said.

She watched Coulson being pushed through a doorway. "When I'm wrong, I admit it." She came back to Payne. "I appreciate all the help you gave us. Without you, we would've never nailed him." She stuck out her hand. "Thank you, sir."

Payne smiled and took her hand. "Thank you, Agent DelaCruz." He paused. "I suppose we got off on the wrong foot back in my office. I'm sorry for my part in all of that." He let go of her hand. "If my assistance is needed in the future, please don't be afraid to ask." His eyes drifted to the table. He sat and put Coulson's untouched food in front of him. "In the meantime, it would be a shame to let this jumbo shrimp go to waste." He gestured toward the booth on the other side of the table. "Would you care to join me?"

Cruz chuckled. "No, thank you." She crossed her ankle over her knee and pulled off one shoe. "The sooner I get out of these heels and into a hot bath the better."

Pastor Lisa Jenkins stepped away from the lectern and approached the front row of wooden pews in the chapel at Hill and Hill Funeral Home. She bent over at the waist and extended her hand straight out, palm down. Smiling, she spoke to the blonde-haired girl, sandwiched between the girl's grandparents. "Would you like to say the prayer with me, Madison?"

Jason and Jane Wilson had been cremated yesterday. Their remains rested in two matching pewter urns atop two wooden pedestals at the front of the chapel. Behind the urns, large photos of the deceased had been placed on stands. Flowers from friends and co-workers surrounded the pictures and remains.

Madison's grandparents worked with the funeral director to have a service for their daughter and son-in-law. They thought the best thing to do was to have a memorial service near the town where the two had worked, so those who knew them could say their goodbyes. Jason's parents had passed away and he was an only child, so he had no living relatives who could pay their respects. Madison's grandparents also made the decision to keep her parents together and take the urns back to Florida. When the girl was older, she could decide what she wanted to do with her parent's ashes.

Sitting in the pews behind Madison and her grandparents, a modest gathering of people who knew the Wilsons, mostly co-workers, waited for her final answer.

Madison whipped her head left and right, getting smiles and nods of approval from her grandparents. She focused on the middle-aged woman with short and graying hair, her attention going back and forth from the woman's face to her outstretched hand. The woman's eyes seemed larger than normal behind the thick lenses of the wire-rimmed eyeglasses perched on her nose.

Pastor Jenkins tipped her head toward the photos and whispered, "Come on, I could use your help."

Clutching her favorite stuffed animal, Froggy, Madison slinked out of the wooden seat, the hem of her pink dress catching on something and rising above her butt, showing her white flowered underwear. Grandma stretched out both hands, but was too late. Her granddaughter was gone. Snickers and giggles drew the attention of Pastor Jenkins, who straightened the dress.

Standing to the side of the urns, Jenkins picked up Madison and held her in the crook of her left arm. She dipped her forehead toward the girl. "Are you ready?" She watched the youngster spy the people before coming back to her and nodding her whole body. Jenkins had to react quickly to keep from getting head-butted. The pastor faced forward and looked to the floor. "Let us bow our heads for the final prayer and blessing."

Madison brought her right arm out from behind Jenkins's neck. "You have to do *this* first." She made the sign of the cross, touching her forehead, chest, left and right shoulder with her fingertips before making eye contact with a woman seated on the end of the pew, next to her grandmother.

Wearing a long-sleeved gray sweater over a black knee-length dress, Special Agent Cruz returned the little girl's smile. Her left eye filled with fluid, but she kept the teardrop from escaping. She winked at Madison and made the sign of the cross.

"Okay then," said Jenkins, who imitated Madison and urged the people to do the same. "Heavenly Father, we commend to you your children, Jason and Jane. Wipe away their tears and their sorrow and give to them unimaginable joy and peace for all eternity." She paused and opened one eye to see the girl in her arms. "Lord, wrap your loving arms around this angel," she bounced Madison on her hip and the girl smiled, "and hold her close to your heart, especially in the coming days and months." Jenkins closed her eyes. "Bless us *all*, Lord, and help us find peace, remembering our loved ones with fondness. In Jesus' name, we pray. Amen."

And, all the people said, "Amen."

When the service concluded, people mulled around, offering condolences to the grandparents and saying goodbye to Madison, until she spotted a man and bolted the length of the chapel. All eyes followed the girl and her trail of verbal Ash's, as she mispronounced the shortened version of Special Agent Ashford's name. He had arrived late and sat in the back, not wanting to disrupt the service.

"Hello, Madison," he said, dropping to one knee and embracing her. "I brought you something."

Watching the two interact, Cruz smiled from ear to ear. Feeling a hand on her shoulder, she turned and saw Mr. and Mrs. Telfor, Madison's grandparents.

Mrs. Telfor put her hands on Cruz's upper arms. "We just wanted to thank you." She shot a glance toward her husband, who nodded. "Mr. Ashford told us everything and," the woman's voice cracked, "well...you didn't have to do what you did—looking after Maddie, I mean, until we could get here. We really appreciate it. Thank you."

Cruz cupped the woman's elbows. "I mean this from the bottom of my heart, Mrs. and Mrs. Telfor—"

"Please," Mrs. Telfor put an arm around her husband's waist, "call us by our first names."

"Thank you. Louise," Cruz shifted her eyes, "Bob, believe me when I say it was *pure joy* spending time with Maddie." She cranked her head around to see her partner horsing around with the girl. Coming back to the Telfors, she added, "You have nothing to fear. Those who sought the child's life are dead...or imprisoned. You're all safe now."

Cruz took turns and hugged Bob and Louise, telling them how sorry she was for their loss. While still in Louise's embrace, Cruz felt a tug on her dress.

"Look what Ash gave me, Raychel."

Cruz went to both knees and leaned back on her haunches. "What is that?"

Madison held up a book. "It's a book about Chilled." She opened it. "It has Annie and Annabelle and Ogar— he's my favorite." She giggled. "He's so funny."

Cruz lifted her eyes. Ashford had walked up behind Madison. "Wow, that Ash...he's so thoughtful." She half grinned at her partner. "He surprises me more and more every day."

Ashford slightly tilted his head and offered a one-shoulder shrug.

Madison lowered the book and stared at Cruz. "Raychel, are you coming with Nana and Buppa and me to Florida?"

Cruz's eyes darted from Ashford to Bob and Louise before settling on the little girl. "No, I can't, Maddie. I have a home and a job here." She saw the happiness drain from Madison's face. The girl's head sunk, and Cruz felt her chest tighten.

"But, why?" cried Madison, her arms hanging limp in front of her body. The book slipped from her grasp and dropped to the floor.

Picking up the book and pulling the girl closer, Cruz hugged the child and stroked the back of her head. "Don't cry, Sweetie. Everything's going to be fine. Your Nana and Buppa love you very much and they're going to take good care of you." She held Madison tightly, gently rocking her back and forth. For a split-second, she thought about moving to Florida. She felt Ashford take the book from her hand. She kissed the top of the girl's head and patted her back with the freed hand. "It's okay, Maddie. You're going to be all right."

A few minutes later, the girl pushed on Cruz's chest, creating only enough separation to stick her stuffed animal between them. Madison sniffed. "Here," she wiped her nose with her palm before Ashford handed her his handkerchief, "I want you to have Froggy."

Cruz's hands enveloped the tiny hands holding the frog. "Thank you, Sweetheart, but I can't take your favorite animal." She wiped the frog's nose across Madison's face, tickling her. "Besides, Froggy would miss you."

Madison crinkled her nose and mouth before drawing her thin eyebrows down as far as she could. "You said *friends do stuff like that for each other,*" the girl looked down and raised the gold chain, pinching the crucifix between her thumb and forefinger, "when you gave me this."

Cruz's head plummeted. The tightness in her chest

     DEFENSE OF INNOCENTS

rose. She swallowed, but her throat seized, making an audible gulp. She pressed her thumb and forefinger against her eyelids before dragging the hand down her face and looking at Madison. Flicking her eyes downward, she put two fingers on the handkerchief in the girl's hand. Her response blended with laughter and crying, she said, "I think I need this, too. Do you mind if I borrow it?"

Cruz wiped her eyes and nose with the white cotton fabric. Placing both hands on her thighs, she raised her shoulders to her neck and held them there for a few seconds before letting them fall and emptying her lungs. "You're absolutely right, Maddie." She took the frog and regarded the stuffed animal for what it was—an expression of love. Cruz curled her hand around the back of Madison's neck and pulled, until their foreheads came together and their noses touched. "Thank you. I'll put Froggy on my bed," she lifted the stuffed animal, "and every night I'll see him and think of you."

A few seconds later, Cruz kissed Madison's forehead and stood. Staring at the girl, she pursed her lips and gently tapped them with her forefinger. "You know, Maddie...Florida isn't that far from Washington, D.C."

Madison tipped her head back, her eyes wide and eyebrows high.

"Would it be okay if I came and visited you from time to time?" She glanced at the Telfor's and their beaming faces. Her question had been for them, too.

Madison charged and wrapped both hands around Cruz's legs, squeezing the woman as hard as she could.

— Thank You —

Thank you for purchasing and reading *Defense of Innocents*. I hope you enjoyed this FBI thriller. But the action continues.

Keep reading for a sneak peek at *Plea for Justice*, the next book in the Special Agent Cruz series.

Blessings and Peace,

Alex

P.S. Don't forget your FREE ebook, *Escape & Evade*, at my website (AlexAnderNovelist.com).

PLEA FOR JUSTICE

AN FBI THRILLER

ALEX ANDER

Excerpt from Plea for Justice

April 15TH; 9:48 P.M.
Norfolk, Virginia

The door opened a crack. Drooping between the edge of the door and the wood frame, the cheap gold-colored chain provided the occupants an illusion of security. Anyone capable of lifting a leg could detach the tiny screws affixing the latch to the door. An eye emerged, centered in the crack and an inch above the bowed chain. The round eye was reduced to a sliver, the brow overhead curving inward toward a partially obstructed long and slim nose. A woman's voice, hoarse and raspy from either, too little sleep, or too many cigarettes mumbled, "What do *you* want?"

"Not *what...whom*, Gina." Jessica Devlin tilted her head to the left and went to her tiptoes. "I'm here to speak with Billy."

"He's not here." Gina's eye glanced at the floor. "He split about a month ago."

"Is that so? Then, how come I saw his truck parked out front?"

Gina twisted her head. A second later, her eye was back.

"Open the door, Gina, so we can talk like civilized

people."

"I don't think that's a good idea."

"Why's that? Is it because you're hiding Billy?"

The eye narrowed again. "I told you, we split. He's long gone and I'm glad. He never treated me right anyway."

"I was hoping we could do this the easy way, but if I have to I can come back with a lot more people. We'll trash the place. You know what'll happen. Is that what you want? I don't—" Devlin heard a commotion further inside the fourth floor apartment and shot to her tiptoes again. "Who's in there with you, Gina?"

"It's...probably just my cat."

"I thought you were allergic to cats." Devlin caught a glimpse of a man's face and shouted, "Stop right there, Billy. Don't you take another—" she watched the man turn his back and bolt across the room, "damn it." She threw back the right half of her black leather jacket and grasped the butt of a forty-five caliber 1911. "Open the door, Gina...*now*." The handgun cleared the holster and Devlin lowered her stance. "If you don't, then you'd better step back...one way or another I'm coming in."

The apartment door behind Devlin swung inward and a man in boxers and a muscle shirt stood in the doorway. Black socks, one slouched at his ankle, completed his ensemble. Scratching the three-day stubble on his cheeks, he used his free hand to scratch behind his boxers. "What's with all the noise out here? People are

          Excerpt from Plea for Justice

trying to sleep. Shut the hell—"

Devlin stuck out her left hand and showed the man the object she clutched, her eyes remaining fixed on the woman. "United States Deputy Marshal, sir. Go back inside. This doesn't concern you." The door slammed behind her. "Make up your mind, Gina. You've got two seconds." Devlin dipped her shoulder.

"All right, all right," screamed Gina, while closing the door. The chain dragged across the latch before the door opened to reveal a short woman with straight, greasy hair plastered to her head. Her ears poked through the stringy strands, giving her the look of a hobbit. Dark rings encircled the woman's eyes. She was wearing a white, off-white or gray bathrobe. The original color would have been a mystery to everyone but the manufacturer and the owner. The woman pressed her body against the wall.

Devlin rushed into the apartment, heading in the direction she had seen Billy running.

"Don't hurt him," cried Gina. "He didn't do nothing."

Devlin did a cursory search of the visible area to make sure the room was clear. Reaching an open window on the far side of the dwelling, she leaned out and yanked her head back inside. She was unsure if Billy had a gun; however, there was no need to give him a target. She heard a crash on the fire escape ladder. After holstering her weapon and sneaking another look, she climbed out the window and descended the stairs.

Getting to the second floor, she leaned over the

railing and saw Billy and the retractable ladder moving in unison. "You know I'm going to catch you, Billy." She propelled her body around the landing and took the steps two and three at a time. "And, when I do, you're going to wish you'd stopped." She hit the last landing at full speed, grabbed the handrail and hurled her body away from the fire escape. The block-style two-inch heels of her black knee boots caught the third rung. She leapt off the ladder and dropped halfway down, grabbing another rung to stop her momentum. Repeating the movement two times more, she hit the concrete, spun on her heels and took off down the alley.

Her heart pounding, Devlin took a hard right at the end of the alley. Water splashed from a puddle when she drove off her left foot and sprinted down the sidewalk. She saw the back of Billy's shirt, a black t-shirt sporting the name of some rock band she did not know.

Billy glanced over his shoulder, his eyes wide. The muscles in his face straining. Turning back around, he collided with a woman, who was focused on the phone in her hand. She spun around and the cell flew out of her hands. Profanity followed.

Devlin dodged and weaved around people. Twisting her five-feet, ten-inch athletic figure, she squeezed between two young lovers and apologized over her shoulder. Bobbing her head left and right, she spotted her prey when a group of teenagers entered a café. He turned right, going down an adjacent alley. She came to a halt

     Excerpt from Plea for Justice

and looked at the name of the restaurant. A grin flashed across her face, while she rushed into the establishment and ran to the back, her badge in hand. "Excuse me, excuse me." She gently redirected customers out of the way with one hand. The other hand held her badge above her head. "I'm with the Marshal's Service." She sidestepped a waiter, who nearly dumped a tray of food on her patrons in an effort to avoid a collision. "Sorry about that," Devlin called out to the woman.

Entering the kitchen, she bumped into another server. This time, plates crashed to the floor. She had no time to assist the woman, a full dish of a tomato-based entrée running down the woman's white uniform. "I'm so sorry." She ran around the grill and bolted for the other side of the kitchen, making a mental note of the woman's face. *I'll stop back and reimburse her for the loss.* Throwing her hands out in front of her body, Devlin hit the horizontal bar on the door and barreled into the alley.

Gasping for air and thinking he had lost his pursuer, Billy had slowed to a jog. When the door to his right swung open, he realized he was wrong. He accelerated to a sprint. A quarter of the way down the alley, he reached for his stomach, while his other arm continued to pump. His pace slackened and he doubled over before stopping. Bent over at the waist with both arms wrapped around his belly, Billy took huge gulps of air. Cocking his head, he saw the dark outline of a tall woman silhouetted against a streetlamp. She looked like the all-black stickers on the back windows of pickup trucks. Instead of posing provocatively like the stickers, she strode toward him. Above the car horns honking in the distance, he heard the heels of her boots making contact with the concrete.

"I told you I'd catch you, Billy."

He straightened. "How'd you..." He took a deep breath and exhaled.

Devlin jerked her thumb behind her. "I knew this alley passed behind the kitchen." Her heart rate had returned to normal. Chalk up the quick recovery time to a strict weekly exercise regimen of kickboxing and jogging. "I had a hunch you'd try to double back for your truck."

"Son of a..." Billy studied the alley ahead of him before coming back to the Deputy Marshal. His eyes darted left and right. He sized up the federal agent. His strength was coming back to him and the flaming sensation in his sides had subsided. He recalled his most recent stint in jail. *I'm not going back—not now, not ever again.*

Devlin ambled toward Billy, producing a pair of handcuffs from under her jacket. "Is it going to be the easy way or the—"

Billy whirled around and took off like a sprinter out of a starting block. He had not run ten steps before he felt his body floating through the air. His left side hit a metal dumpster, sending a burning pain up his arm. He bounced backward, but stayed on his feet, only to be

     Excerpt from Plea for Justice

driven into the side of the metal box again. His lips kissed the edge of the container. He smelled the remains of last night's dinner, only the stench made his stomach churn.

With her forearm pressed against Billy's neck and her hand full of t-shirt, Devlin thrust her knee between his thighs and wrenched the man's right arm behind his back. "If you move, I'll knock your teeth out." She locked the handcuffs around his wrists, took a step backward and ran the fingers of one hand through her jet-black medium-length straight hair. Letting out a visible breath of the cool night air, she tilted her head and gazed at the stars. "Why do you always choose the hard way, Billy? Just once it would be nice..." she rotated her head. Somewhere down the alley, an empty bottle rolled across the pavement. Four figures materialized from the shadows and closed the distance. One twirled a baseball bat, possibly a club, while another dragged a chain along the concrete behind him.

Excerpt from Plea for Justice

The men fanned out and surrounded Devlin in a half-circle. The chain man stood to the right. On the left was baseball bat. The two in the middle appeared to be unarmed. The dark-skinned Latino directly in front of her wore a tattered and dingy muscle shirt, baggy shorts that came below his knees and white high-end tennis shoes in immaculate condition. The man hoisted his shorts. Letting them go, they immediately fell back down. If it weren't for the weapons in play, Devlin would have laughed and told them to get lost.

"Hola chiquita," said Shorts in a Spanish accent. "Who you supposed to be?" He gave her an exaggerated scan and added, "Some sexy superhero—all dressed in black." He looked to his gang and received the adulation he was expecting. "Hey sexy superhero, how about you come over here and give me a kiss." More laughter ensued.

Devlin saw Shorts motion toward himself, but the spot he picked was not his lips.

Billy pivoted away from the dumpster. "This chick's crazy, dudes. Help me out. She's—"

Her eyes never straying from Shorts, Devlin grabbed a handful of Billy's hair and shoved his face into the trash container. "Quiet Billy, while I speak to these gentlemen." She paused, her muscles tense. Never letting go of Billy's slick mop, she moved her right hand to her midsection. "I have no issue with you boys." She dipped her head slightly, staring down Shorts. "Let's keep it that way."

"Ooh, damn girl," mocked Shorts. He pointed a curved finger at Devlin, accentuating the gesture with his whole body. "You got some *big ones*, coming into *our turf* and disrespecting us like that. In case you haven't noticed," he used the same curved finger to include the men around him, "it's four against one." He laughed and took a step closer. "I'll take those odds any day."

"I wouldn't, *punk*." Devlin peeled back her jacket and cleared the 1911 from its holster. The muzzle went straight for Shorts' nose. "Your boys brought chains and baseball bats to a gun fight. Not too smart, *homey*."

Shorts froze. The hole at the end of the gun was bigger and blacker than the night sky. After a quick sideways glance at his crew, he recovered his manhood and crossed his arms over his chest. Cocking his head off to one side and jerking a thumb toward the man to his right, he smirked and said, "Who says *we* don't have guns?"

Devlin squinted. "That's why you two will be the *first* to die." The realization of potential imminent death wiped the sneer from Shorts' face. The darkness provided the perfect backdrop for Devlin to see the color drain from the man's cheeks. His shoulders slumped and the expanded chest sunk. She whipped her head to the right.

"Let go of the chain." The man hesitated. "Drop it now or I swing the hand cannon your way." He complied and she went back to staring at Shorts. "You there...Louisville Slugger...I want to hear the sound of wood bouncing off the—" the bat resounded off the hard surface, hitting a few times before coming to rest, "...pavement."

Devlin let go of Billy, kicked him in the back of the knees and he dropped to the concrete. "Have a seat, Billy and don't go anywhere. We're not done." Taking a two-handed grip on the forty-five, she motion for Louisville Slugger and Chain to join his friends. "I want all of you to get the hell out of here," the pistol swayed left and right, encompassing all of them, "before I arrest you for..." she paused, "for *something*. But, before you leave, let me give you a piece of advice." She pointed the weapon at the crotch of Shorts, who reflexively crossed his hands in front of his groin. "If you're going to act tough...for crying out loud, pull up your pants. Who's going to take you seriously with your shorts hanging down below your crack?"

Shorts glanced at his fellow gangbangers. They twisted their faces and shrugged.

She motioned with her head. "Get out of here." They started to take off down the alley toward the kitchen door Devlin had exited. "Not that way, boys." She waved the gun in the opposite direction. "Head back the way you came and crawl back into your hole." Once they were gone, she holstered her weapon and helped Billy get to a sitting position, his back to the rusting dumpster.

"You broke my tooth," he said, the last word sounding like 'toof.'

"As I said I would if you jerked me around." She held out her hands and raised her shoulders. "None of this had to happen, Billy. I just wanted to talk. There was no warrant for your arrest. You weren't in trouble. But, you ran." She tapped the badge on her belt. "And, because I wear one of these, I have a duty to chase anyone who flees from me."

"I didn't do nothing." Once again, the letter 'F' sounded in the last word. He was tired. His tooth was aching and he was on the verge of tears.

Devlin felt sorry for him. Every word she had said to him was true. People like Billy, however, panic when they see a law enforcement officer. They have been in trouble with the law so much they automatically think they did something wrong and run. It was the nature of the beast. She approached him, squatted and sat on her haunches. She smiled and spoke to him in a calm tone, almost as if she were speaking to a small child. "I just need some information from you and you can go." She shook her head. "No strings attached...I promise." She gave him time to compose himself. "Tell me where I can find Tony Fusco."

     Excerpt from Plea for Justice

www.ingramcontent.com/pod-product-compliance
Lightning Source LLC
Chambersburg PA
CBHW022001120726

47992CB00001B/362